THE W SERIES (BOOK 4)

TRACIE DELANEY

Copyright © 2017 Tracie Delaney

Content Editing by *Jessica Anderegg - Red Adept Editing*
Line Editing by *Sarah Carleton - Red Adept Editing*
Cover art by *Art by Karri*

All rights reserved. No part of this publication may be reproduced, stored in any retrieval system, or transmitted, in uniform or by any means, electronic, mechanical, photocopying, recording or otherwise without prior written permission of the author.

This is a work of fiction. Names, characters, places, and incidents are either the products of the author's imagination or are used fictitiously, and any resemblance to actual persons, living or dead, business establishments, events, or locales is entirely coincidental.

For Louise - my rock

1

Something wasn't right. Not only did he have the mother of all hangovers, but a sour smell hung in the air as well.

Groggy with sleep, Rupe opened his eyes a crack. Oak bedside cabinet? No, his was mahogany, and he didn't have an ugly old lamp set on top of it.

He touched the sheets and felt stiff polyester instead of one-thousand-thread hand-stitched Egyptian cotton.

He forced his eyes open a little wider. He could just make out a sign on the back of the door. Did it say "In Case of Fire"?

His brain was foggy, as though it had been stuffed full of cotton wool that prevented it from working properly. He kept getting flashes of the previous night but no clear images. The club. Shots lined up on the bar. The pounding bass beat of the music. Nessa clinging to him like a wet towel.

Christ, that's right. He'd been clubbing with Nessa.

He groaned and tried to turn his head. The splitting pain in his temples from such a simple movement stopped that plan in its tracks. As he dragged himself closer to consciousness, he had a vague recollection of Nessa suggesting they go back to her hotel room. Yet he had absolutely no memory of actually getting there, or what they'd got up to when they arrived. Given how bad he felt, he wouldn't be surprised if he'd passed out before his dick had gone anywhere near her. If that was the case, she'd be royally pissed off.

He patted the sheets behind him but came up empty. Had she already left? He rolled onto his back, groaning as the movement made it feel as though his brain was slamming against the sides of his skull. He winced and held his breath, waiting for the searing pain to sod off.

As the spasms receded, he reached out his arm again. This time, he touched flesh. *Damn.* She was still there. He hated the morning after, even with Nessa, who he quite liked. The fact she was married made him like her more. No chance of any awkward questions about where the relationship was going. Still, he preferred it when whoever he'd chosen to spend the night with left before he woke. It was easier that way.

"Hey," he rasped, his voice sounding as if he'd swallowed several razor blades that had then sliced through his vocal cords. "Nessa, you awake?"

When she didn't reply, he ordered his eyes to bloody well open up. After a few seconds of negotiation, they obeyed.

Nessa was still fast asleep, her skin a pallid yellow. Poor bugger. She would feel as rough as he did when she came to, especially given how much she'd drunk at the club.

"Hey," he said again, accompanying his words with a brief shake of her arm. Her body was cold, mottled. He shook harder, a sense of unease creeping across his skin, causing the hairs on the back of his neck to stand on end. He sat up, and his stomach protested at the sudden violent movement. He managed to make it to the wastebasket—just.

On wobbly legs, he staggered back to the bed, working his way to Nessa's side. He loomed over her.

"Oh God, no." The words erupted from him of their own

accord. No forethought. His blood turned to ice in his veins. He had zero experience with dead people.

Until that moment.

With a trembling hand, he pressed two fingers to her neck even though he knew the result already. No pulse. *What the actual fuck?* A cold sensation crept over every single one of his vertebrae, and his stomach lurched again.

Holy shit. He'd slept next to a dead woman.

Nessa was dead. *How can Nessa be dead?*

How long had she been dead? How had she died? *What do I do now?*

Calm down, Witters. He hated the nickname his best mate, Cash, had given him when they'd met at school twenty-odd years ago, but somehow, the familiarity alleviated his growing panic.

He took a deep breath through his nose, holding the air down in his lungs until they burned. Slowly, slowly, he breathed out before repeating the process three times.

Feeling more composed, he quickly dressed. He picked up his phone. *Damn.* He didn't know where he was. He scanned the room, his eyes alighting on the hotel directory next to the TV.

Baroque Hotel.

Where the hell was that?

He stabbed the name into Google and wrote down the street address before opening the hotel door. Room 422. With clammy hands, he called the police.

The boys in blue took less than fifteen minutes to arrive. He'd bet if he'd called about a burglary, he'd still be waiting for them a week later. A dead body, however, was a lot more interesting—though to him, it was a nightmare.

"Mr Fox-Whittingham." The lead copper shook Rupe's hand. "I'm Officer Davies." He pointed to his colleague. "This is Officer Sullivan. You called us about a body?"

The copper's casual delivery, as though he were talking about fixing Rupe's guttering or selling double glazing, left Rupe amazed.

"Come in," he muttered.

Right behind the police, a couple of paramedics carrying a stretcher headed straight over to Nessa. Rupe glanced over his shoulder and shuddered.

"We just need to ask you a few questions," Davies said.

"Sure." Rupe waved a hand at the only two chairs in the room. He remained standing, his back to the bed. He could hear the paramedics busying themselves behind him, and he tried to shut his mind off from the reality of what they were doing.

Davies took out a small notebook and a pencil. "Can you tell us the deceased's name?"

Rupe grimaced. "Vanessa Reynolds."

"And how long have you known Miss Reynolds?"

"Mrs Reynolds."

The officers shared a look. Rupe bristled and pulled himself upright. "Don't tell me you've never shagged a married woman, Officer Davies. Or at least wished you had."

A tinge of pink touched Davies's cheeks. "My apologies, Mr Fox-Whittingham."

Rupe took pity on the young guy. He only looked to be in his midtwenties. *Probably his first dead body.* Rupe almost laughed. It was his first dead body, too, and hopefully his last.

"I've known her about a year, on and off. More off than on, if you catch my drift."

Officer Davies cleared his throat. "And did you spend the whole evening here in the hotel room?"

Rupe tried to focus. He dug his fingertips into his temples and massaged in circles. "Sorry, terrible hangover. No. We went to a club. The Vault, I think. At least that's where I usually go when I'm in London. I honestly can't remember. The head bouncer knows me, so he'll be able to tell you if I was there."

"I see. And were you and Mrs Reynolds with anyone else?"

"I usually meet up with a few acquaintances when I'm in town. No one stands out. I had a lot to drink."

The officers shared another look. Davies scribbled with his pencil, the scratching noise against the paper like a pneumatic drill boring through Rupe's skull. Didn't all coppers use iPads now? The whoosh of a nylon belt strap being pulled through a buckle made him look over his shoulder. The paramedics had transferred Nessa to a gurney and were strapping her in. His stomach churned, and Davies's voice faded into the background. How did a young, seemingly healthy woman simply croak in the middle of the night?

"Mr Fox-Whittingham." Davies's sharp voice broke through his reverie.

"Sorry, what?" Rupe frowned.

"Maybe it's better if we do this down at the station. Would you mind accompanying us?"

Rupe's eyes widened. "Am I under arrest?"

"No, no, not at all. It's routine. We need a statement from you, and, if I may say, you seem a little distracted. Not at all surprising, given the circumstances," Davies added quickly when Rupe fixed him with a stare.

"Sure." He shrugged. "Which station? I'll follow you down."

Davies raised an eyebrow. "We'll give you a lift. Probably not a good idea to be arrested for drunk driving, Mr Fox-Whittingham."

Rupe gave him a faint smile. "Fair point."

Davies stood, followed by Sullivan, who hadn't said a word. Rupe briefly wondered why he had come, unless travelling in pairs was routine. He snatched his jacket off the back of the chair and followed the officers into the hallway. Rupe closed the door behind him, leaving the paramedics tending to the dead body.

Rupe woke to find he'd slept all day. It hadn't taken very long to give his statement, and as soon as he arrived home, he flopped onto the sofa and passed out. The living room was cast in darkness, and the coffee cold in the mug beside him. He moved his head slowly. No stabbing pain. At least his hangover had fucked off. His stomach rumbled painfully—not surprising, given that he hadn't eaten all day, although for many hours, food had been the last thing on his mind.

He wandered into the kitchen and opened the fridge. His housekeeper was off that day, but she hadn't let him down. The fridge was jammed full of freshly prepared food, all labelled with heating instructions and use-by dates. Abi was a bloody marvel.

He spied a portion of Abi's super-healthy chicken curry at the back and rearranged the fridge until he could reach it and pull it out. He turned the dial on the oven to the right temperature, opened the door, and shoved the foil carton inside.

He scoffed the lot, even though the portion size would easily have fed two. He'd go to the gym the next day and work it off. After years of being on the burly side—Cash would say *fat*, which was unfair—he'd finally succumbed to a life of healthy eating and gruelling workouts. After the first few months, he'd discovered he actually liked going to the gym, helped no doubt by the fact it was full of smoking-hot women. And although his sex life before hadn't exactly been on the meagre side, he had to admit that toned abs worked wonders for attracting the ladies.

His thoughts turned to Nessa. *Poor bitch*. But did she have to breathe her last on the day he'd bedded her? He cursed, kicking himself for such a selfish thought. At least she didn't have kids. Her marriage was a sham, one of convenience rather than love, as she'd repeated to him on more than one occasion. He shuddered, his skin crawling as he thought back to spending the night next to a corpse.

The following morning, he felt a lot better, and after a workout at the gym and three regular meals, the horror of the previous night began to recede. The police hadn't called with any news, although he didn't expect them to. He wasn't even a witness. He'd heard nothing, seen nothing, knew nothing.

As the evening drew in, Rupe settled in front of the TV, a beer bottle dangling between his fingers. The All Blacks were playing the Lions. The game had been on for about ten minutes when a loud banging on the door interrupted his viewing pleasure.

Rupe climbed off the couch and went to answer the door. As he walked down the hallway, whoever was outside banged again.

"Hang on, will you?" Rupe shouted as he slid back the bolts. He drew open the door. Outside stood two guys, suited and booted. They both thrust their identity cards in his face.

"Mr Fox-Whittingham. We need you to come to the station with us, please, sir."

Rupe frowned as he glanced at the cards. "What's this about?"

"We have some questions, sir, about the death of Mrs Vanessa Reynolds."

Rupe shook his head in irritation. "I already gave you my statement yesterday."

"Yes, sir. I am aware. I'm afraid we need to ask you some more questions."

A feeling of dread started at the base of Rupe's spine and crept upwards until it curled around his neck like a scarf—one that was beginning to cut off his air supply.

"Am I under arrest?"

The detective gave a smile that didn't reach his eyes. "No, sir. Just helping us with our enquiries."

"And if I refuse?"

"*Then* you'll give me no choice but to arrest you."

2

Jayne shifted the enormous stack of files in her arms to her left hip and managed to remove her keys from her bag without dropping them. A minor miracle. She unlocked the door to her apartment and kicked it open.

After dropping the heap of papers on the dining room table, she headed straight for the fridge. She opened it, and a smile of relief crept across her lips. Putting a bottle of Sauvignon Blanc in to chill before she'd left for work that morning had been nothing short of miraculous foresight, especially as she'd had to work the previous weekend to try and make a dent in her enormous caseload. Divorce made for good business—as her own divorce lawyer could attest to.

She poured herself a glass, and after two or three sips, the slug of anxiety in her gut began to dissipate. She sank into her favourite chair next to a floor-to-ceiling picture window with a fabulous view of the river. The view—along with the open-plan style, which made the room big enough for her beloved dining room table—had been the clincher when she'd chosen the apartment, even if the place was ridiculously expensive for having only one bedroom and three hundred square feet of living space.

She kicked off her shoes and tucked up her feet. Her latest case would be the death of her. Something didn't smell right with the wife's story, and Jayne had learned over the years to trust her instincts. They rarely let her down.

Unlike husbands and best friends.

She shook her head. Nope. Not going there. Not tonight. She needed to be kind to herself after the week she'd had. Wine, case review, bubble bath, bed. In that order.

With a deep sigh, she got up and picked the first folder off the top of the enormous pile that was mocking her from the dining room table. She sat back down, opened it, and began to read. Occasionally, she made notes in the margin. The remainder of the time, she tapped her pen against her teeth, a habit her partner at work hated—which made her do it more often. She and Darren loved to wind each other up.

After her much-needed bath, Jayne slipped on her nightgown and traipsed to bed. She'd just snuggled beneath the covers when her phone rang. She cursed as she realised she'd left it in the next room. She tossed back the covers and went to fetch it. By the time she reached the living room, the phone had stopped ringing. It immediately started up again, and a prick of anxiety gnawed at her insides. What if something was wrong with Ganny? She flipped the phone over and stared at the screen.

Kyle.

Well, he could sod off. It was late. She was tired and cranky and not up to whatever games her soon-to-be ex-husband wanted to play. She turned and was ready to head back to bed when her phone beeped with an incoming text. *Just ignore it.* Kyle loved sending her nasty texts, especially when she wouldn't bend to his will.

But curiosity got the better of her. She swiped at the screen, and the message appeared: *I know you're there. Answer your bloody phone, Jayne.*

Jayne glanced around. She wouldn't put anything past Kyle,

including spying on her. He'd assured her he didn't have a key and had given her the only one when she'd kicked him out over nine months ago, but she didn't trust him. Someone who would screw his wife's best friend and barely break stride when caught was not a man to be trusted.

The fact he'd shagged Flick was bad enough. That he'd done it over the antique table that Jayne's beloved grandfather had left her in his will was unforgivable. He might as well have pissed on her grandfather's grave. And as for her best friend... Jayne's heart squeezed painfully. Despite the time that had passed, she still missed Flick like crazy. They'd been friends for years, and yet Flick had betrayed Jayne in the worst possible way. It seemed loyalty was about as rare as the bloody dodo.

Jayne went to switch off her phone but then hesitated. She had to be contactable at all times in case Ganny needed her. She'd never forgive herself if something happened to her grandmother and she hadn't been reachable.

Another text pinged, and Jayne sighed as she opened and read it: *Fine, play your stupid games. I'll call by tomorrow on my way to work. Be in, Jayne.*

She bristled with anger. Who the hell did he think he was? She'd never taken well to orders, even when she was married and still in the besotted stage. Now that they were on the cusp of divorce, he could piss off if he thought for one minute she'd bend to his will.

Kyle was a man of habit. He'd turn up precisely at seven the next morning, expecting to see her.

She'd be out the door by six thirty.

THE FOLLOWING MORNING, Jayne left home half an hour before Kyle was due to arrive, but instead of heading straight to work, she ducked into the café opposite her apartment block and grabbed a table by the window. She ordered a coffee and a granola yoghurt pot and settled in for her morning's entertainment.

Since Kyle's betrayal, something had changed inside her. The job had hardened her over the years, and early on, she'd learned to protect her heart by building a wall around it, but being cheated on had turned the bricks into steel. Impenetrable. Kyle's deception had also made her belligerent, especially when it came to her dealings with him. Whatever Kyle demanded, she dug in her heels. He wanted a quickie divorce. She put every obstacle in his way. He wanted to sell the apartment and split the proceeds. She hired the best property-dispute lawyer and tied him in enough red tape to encircle the earth. Twice. She cleared out their joint account and cancelled their credit cards, which resulted in a very embarrassing incident for Kyle at a Michelin-starred restaurant in Mayfair.

And yet she was far from completely blameless in the breakdown of her marriage—not that she would *ever* admit as much to Kyle.

She'd be pressured to compromise in the end. The legal system would always come down on the side of fair and equitable, and although Kyle hadn't put as much financially into their marriage as she had, his contribution would still be recognised—which pissed her off. He earned a fifth of what she did, and yet, with a sympathetic judge, he could get half of everything. Her assets, her savings, her pension. Not if she had anything to do with it, though. Kyle had labelled her as a woman scorned. She might as well live up to stereotypes. It would be such a shame to disappoint him.

As reliable as Big Ben, Kyle appeared outside her apartment block at two minutes before seven, meaning he'd be at her door by seven on the dot. She'd once thought his extreme consistency and habit of being a stickler for punctuality were endearing. These days, she found it odd at best, annoying at worst. It was as if his adultery had taken the blinkers off of her and she could see the real man beneath the veneer. It wasn't a pretty sight.

She sipped her coffee, her lips twitching as she predicted he'd be banging on her door right about then, furious she wasn't answering. She counted in her head, and at 7:03 he appeared, red faced, a deep scowl marring features she'd once found handsome.

He planted his hands on his hips and looked up and down the street. Jayne smiled to herself. His fury was evident in his posture and expression. *Too bad, dickhead. You messed with the wrong girl.*

He removed his phone from the inside pocket of his jacket and stabbed his fingers at the screen. Jayne waited. Sure enough, a few seconds later, her phone pinged. She reached into her bag.

The message read, "You'll pay for this, Jayne."

Oh yeah? How?

Kyle stomped up the road towards the tube station. He rounded the corner and disappeared from view.

Jayne finished her coffee, left a tip on the table, and set off for work. That little entertaining diversion had set her up to have a great day.

She arrived at work with a smile on her face, the complete opposite of the previous day's demeanour when her scowl had scored her forehead so deeply that Darren had suggested Botox. Only the once, mind. She'd perfected the death stare for Kyle and found it worked on most men.

Donna, her PA, had her coffee waiting, along with a printed copy of her calendar for the day. Jayne gave her a grateful smile, said a bright good morning, and closed the door to her office. She scanned the piece of paper. Busy, busy, busy. She was glad to have little time to think. Having her brain constantly spin around her skull, flashing the occasional unwanted image, was a state of mind to be avoided at all costs. She'd discovered maxing out on work was a good strategy for curbing the undesirable thoughts, hence her current sixteen-hour day schedule.

She sank into her leather chair and perched her reading glasses on the end of her nose. Varifocals gave her a headache, so the only way to switch from close-up to distance was to assume this ridiculous pose that made her look like her old headmistress.

Jayne began prepping for her first client of the day, but as she made notes of what she needed to discuss with him before their court date a week on Tuesday, a commotion outside her office disturbed her. Jayne was halfway across her office to find out what on earth was going on when the door burst open, and Kyle marched in, face like thunder, with Donna hovering at his shoulder.

"I'm sorry, Jayne," she said. "He wouldn't take no for an answer."

Jayne waved her hand in the air. "It's fine."

Donna discreetly closed the door while Jayne remained standing, hands planted low on her hips.

"What do you want, Kyle?" she said in a bored tone.

"Where the *hell* were you this morning, Jayne? I told you I was coming by."

"So you did." She yawned. "Unfortunately for you, I stopped listening to anything you had to say the minute I found you balls-deep inside my best friend."

Kyle's face reddened, but it wasn't from embarrassment because the blotched skin was accompanied by a thick vein that pulsed in his forehead—a tell of rage Jayne had always found unattractive, even when she'd been infatuated with him.

"Old news, Jayne. Done." He slashed his hand across his throat for added effect. "I know you're still in love with me, but let it go, for both our sakes."

Jayne almost choked. This guy lived in an alternate reality, one inhabited within his own crazed, narcissistic mind. She formed her face into indifference, her shoulders low and loose.

"In love? Sure, sure. I sit at home every night craving your scintillating company and paint-by-numbers approach to sex."

His face furrowed in confusion. "What the hell are you talking about?"

She folded her arms across her chest. "Let's see. Three kisses, one with tongue, followed by a twist of my nipples like you're trying to tune the radio in, a couple of fingers stuffed inside me before I'm treated to being pumped by your half-flaccid cock until you reach orgasm. And after seven years of me guiding you to my clit, you still couldn't find it. Maybe I should have drawn you a map." She shrugged. "Although even then…"

She let her words trail off, her face still fixed with the impassive stare she'd mastered after several years working as a lawyer, even though her heart galloped inside her chest. Being so hostile towards the man she'd once loved and had spent the best years of her life with didn't come easily, but she had to put herself first. Her self-esteem had taken a real battering, and this combative approach was the way she'd chosen to deal with it—rightly or wrongly.

The vein on Kyle's forehead was so pronounced it could almost qualify for citizenship as an independent being. Jayne held back a grin that threatened to bleed across her face. Kyle was useless at comebacks.

"You're a fucking cold bitch."

Yep, and there it was. The stereotypical retort. Jayne allowed a minute curve to her lips. "I know," she said in a condescending tone. "Now, if you don't mind. I'm busy."

She made her way over to her desk and sat down. She picked up her pen and began to make notes on the paperwork in front of her while Kyle's heavy breathing assaulted her ears. After a few seconds of silence, she lifted her chin.

"Anything else?" She hadn't let him share the reason for stopping by her apartment or coming by her office, and her question effectively dismissed him.

Kyle took a menacing step forward, but his faux alpha-male stance didn't worry Jayne. Kyle wasn't the type to hit a woman, and if he tried to, it'd be the last thing he did. Krav Maga worked wonders for getting out aggression—and for learning how to drop a grown man to his knees with one kick or punch.

"Sign the fucking divorce papers, Jayne. I want this over with."

She leaned back in her chair, her pen tapping against her teeth. "I will. As soon as you give up insisting on half. That's *my* apartment, bought with money that *I* earned. *My* pension. *My* savings. Your demands are unreasonable, and I won't give in to them."

Kyle expelled an irritated breath. "I deserve half. All those months and years waiting every night for you to get home and be a *wife*. Instead you chose your career. Even when you were at home, you either had your bloody phone glued to your ear or your head buried in a stack of papers."

Guilt swarmed within her, but she couldn't let it bubble over. Her part in the breakdown of their marriage was something she'd have to examine, but only when she was ready, when the scars on her heart were healed. She called forth her inner bitch to help her respond, even as she inwardly cringed at the cruel words that came out.

"Aww, poor little Kyle. Needs constant attention. Needs his ego stroked at least three times per day." She laughed without mirth. "You chose the wrong woman for that."

"Why do you think I screwed Flick?" he said, his tone bitter and hurt. "At least she knows how to treat a man."

Jayne held back a wince. She wouldn't give him the satisfaction of knowing one of his darts had hit the board. "Depends on your definition of *man*. Flick always did have low self-esteem. No wonder she was flattered by you."

Kyle blanched. "I don't know what I ever saw in you."

Jayne laughed, a proper laugh this time. "Oh, Kyle. The

feeling is mutual. Now, run along. I have work to do. You know my terms. Don't bother me again until you've agreed to them."

She buried her head in her work, and a few seconds later, the door slammed. She looked up. The office was empty. She blew out a heavy breath, her cheeks puffing up. Sparring sessions with Kyle brought out a side of her she didn't like. She wasn't a bitch. Driven, yes. Thoughtless at times, definitely. But she cared about people—her grandmother, friends, colleagues, and clients. Yet she had to fight him. What would it do to her reputation as a top divorce lawyer if her own husband took her to the cleaners?

She took off her glasses and rubbed her eyes.

The door to her office creaked, and Donna poked her head inside. "You okay?"

Jayne nodded. "I can handle Kyle."

"I'm sorry. He just shoved past me. I couldn't stop him."

"No need to apologise." She held up her half-drunk coffee, which had gone cold because of Kyle's interruption. "Would you mind grabbing me another one before my next client arrives?"

Donna smiled warmly. "Coming right up."

Jayne worked right through until nine in the evening. She stood and stretched out her back, her muscles protesting at being stuck in the same position for hours on end. She flicked off the light on her desk, gathered her things together, and locked the door to her office. The hallway was in darkness. Normal, sane people had long ago left for the evening, but as she didn't have any reason to go home, she preferred to work.

Jayne pressed the button for the lift and waited for it to arrive. As she stepped through the open doors, her phone rang. She stepped back into the hallway because the lift would block her signal. She glanced at her phone. Darren.

"Hey," she said warmly. "Everything okay?"

"Sorry to call so late," Darren said. "Are you home yet?"

Jayne laughed. "This is me, remember?"

Darren made a frustrated noise. "You worry me, Jayne."

She smiled to herself. Darren was such a good friend, but he was wasting his time if he thought his disapproval of her working hours would make a difference. "I'm sure you weren't calling to tell me that. What's up?"

"I need a favour. I wouldn't normally ask, but I can't get hold of Peter," he said, referring to their senior partner. "A friend of a friend has got himself in a bit of bother and needs a lawyer to sit with him during police questioning. I'd go, but the baby isn't well."

"Nothing too serious, I hope?" Jayne said, feeling a tinge of concern for Darren's young baby.

"Just a bit of colic, but I don't want to leave Alicia to cope alone."

"I understand. Criminal law isn't really my bag though, Darren."

"I know, but you're not exactly unskilled in that area. It was your second major after all. Look, it's only for the initial questioning. I'll take over if the case goes any further."

Jayne shifted her bag to her opposite shoulder and cleared her throat. She was tired and cranky, and spending hours in a police station was the last thing she wanted, but Darren wouldn't have asked if he'd had any other choice. "Okay," she said. "As it's you."

He laughed. "You're a life saver."

"Hang on. I'm just going back to my office, so I can take proper notes." Jayne strode back down the hallway towards her office and unlocked it then nudged the door open with her hip. She dropped everything she was carrying onto the floor and pulled out her chair. She set her mobile down on the desk and put it on speaker.

"Are you still there?"

"Yes," Darren said.

"Right, give me everything you have."

3

The custody sergeant brought Rupe a weak cup of tea. His mother would have called it *gnats' piss*. He warmed his hands on the paper cup and glanced around the waiting room. How the fuck had he ended up here?

"Has my lawyer arrived yet?"

The sergeant shook his head. "I'll let you know when they get here."

"And then what happens?"

The copper must have taken pity on Rupe, because he stopped on his way to the door. "The detectives in charge of the case will ask their questions."

"And then I'll be free to go?"

The sergeant shrugged. "Maybe," he said, his tone noncommittal.

He closed the door behind him. Rupe took out his phone. The All Blacks had won. He silently cursed and then dropped his phone on the table. He began pacing around the room. *Christ, please let Cash get a decent lawyer here pronto.* He'd seen the looks on the coppers' faces as he'd insisted on legal representation even though they'd made it clear he wasn't under arrest. Rupe was a lot of things—stupid wasn't one of them. He'd given his statement, but as it seemed that wasn't enough, he didn't want to take any chances by talking to seasoned detectives without a smart, experienced criminal lawyer by his side.

His sympathy for Nessa began to ebb away as his own self-preservation came to the fore. He should have stayed in the Caribbean. He sat back down and closed his eyes, imagining the gentle rocking of the boat, the blue-green waters all around, and smoked salmon and champagne on a never-ending conveyor belt.

Where the hell was his bloody lawyer?

JAYNE PAID the cab driver and stepped onto the pavement. Her hair had come loose on the journey over, probably because she kept fiddling with it. She didn't experience nerves at work, but this wasn't exactly her day job. She had also tried Peter's phone several times on the way to the station, but to no avail.

She stuck her bag between her knees and fixed her hair by shoving a couple of extra bobby pins into her chignon. *That should do it.* With a quick glance at her reflection in a nearby window, she lifted her bag onto her shoulder and entered the police station.

The desk sergeant was reading the paper, slouching to the side as he flicked through the pages. He didn't look up as she entered. She was half tempted to ding the bell. Instead, she cleared her throat, and he reluctantly raised his head.

"Can I help you?" he said in a bored tone.

Jayne held back an irritated sigh and pushed her business card across the desk. "I'm here to see my client, Rupert Fox-Whittingham."

The sergeant gave it a cursory glance. "Wait over there," he said, pointing to a row of plastic chairs upon which Jayne had no intention of sitting. He picked up the phone as she paced. Five minutes later, the door to the main body of the station opened, and a detective in his late thirties with a goatee beard, wispy greying hair, and piercing blue eyes walked through.

"Miss Seymour." He thrust out his hand. "Detective Fisher. Would you like to come with me?"

Jayne followed the detective through a wide metal door. It closed behind them with a clang followed by a loud buzzer, denoting that a person was only getting out with approval. She was led to a small, windowless room that had a steel table in the centre and two chairs, both of which looked as comfortable to sit on as a cactus.

"I'll go and get Mr Fox-Whittingham from the waiting area. How long do you think you'll need?" Detective Fisher asked.

Something about the detective's attitude set Jayne's teeth on edge. Maybe it was the air of superiority he projected, or maybe it was his cocky smirk.

She fixed him with a hard stare. "Are you new to the position, Detective Fisher?"

Fisher stiffened his spine at her barely veiled insult. "No."

"Then you'll know I will take as long as necessary and no longer."

Fisher muttered something about cold bitches before he spun on his heel and slammed the door. It was an attitude Jayne was used to, and his comments harmlessly bounced off her like jelly beans thrown at a suit of armour. She eyed the chairs with antipathy before perching on the end of the one facing the door. She liked to get an early first look at any new client, and even though this was a criminal case rather than a civil one, her approach would be the same. Body language could provide a lot of clues about an individual.

She glanced at her watch. *Almost ten o'clock.* Exhaustion swamped her. It was so much more than tiredness, which could be fixed by a good night's sleep. Her fatigue was bone deep. She pinched the bridge of her nose as her eyes briefly closed. She loved her job, but the twenty-four, seven expectations of her clients on top of her own divorce were beginning to take their toll. Her caseload was already horrendous, and yet there she was, taking on another case, albeit only temporarily.

The door handle rattled, and Jayne straightened and sat back, wincing as the metal chair caused a shooting pain through her coccyx. Would it kill the police to provide a bit of cushioning?

As Rupert Fox-Whittingham was led inside, Jayne cast her gaze over him, assessing, judging, and weighing him to see what type of person he was. Her summation: straight as they came.

"Thank you, Detective," she said, effectively dismissing Fisher, who scowled at her before turning his back and leaving the room.

"Mr Fox-Whittingham, I'm Jayne Seymour, your lawyer. Please, take a seat."

Her client lowered himself into the chair opposite, his legs spread wide, hands resting in his lap. And then he slowly grinned —a rather unusual reaction, considering his predicament.

"Well, if you're my reward, I'll happily spend every day of the week being questioned by the police."

4

Rupe could have taken a punch to the gut and it wouldn't have winded him as much as laying eyes on Jayne Seymour had. She put the double *P* in *Prim and Proper*, and she did things to his insides no woman had achieved in thirty-five years. *Goddamn*. Cash had certainly come through for him on the sexy stakes. If she also happened to be a shit-hot lawyer who could get him out of this place, he'd give Cash his firstborn.

"I beg your pardon?" she said, glaring at him with sharp hazel eyes that carried more than a hint of annoyance. The icy stare she bestowed on him didn't remotely dull how utterly gorgeous she was.

He winked at her. The movement was quick—the twitch of an eye—but the delectable Miss Seymour was clearly a woman who paid attention to minute details. She'd noticed the wink. And she bristled.

"Do you know where you are, Mr Fox-Whittingham?"

Oh, he knew all right. He should have been shitting himself, hanging onto her every lawyerly word, and following her instructions to the letter. But when he'd walked into that room and seen perfection right there in the tatty, run-down police station where she was as out of place as he was, it had brought to the fore his usual flippant, devil-may-care attitude. Something about the cold, icy exterior of Jayne Please Let Me Seymour had him forgetting his predicament and wanting to have some fun. *Hmm, wonder if I can break through that armour plating in the time we have available? Probably not, but I'll have a good time trying.*

"Of course I know where I am, darling. I'm at the cop shop."

Jayne sat up straighter in her chair, her irritation with his laissez-faire attitude thinly veiled beneath a professional exterior. "Right, Mr Fox-Whittingham. Let's get started, shall we?"

"Can we cut the Mr Fox-Whittingham malarkey?" The next words were out before Rupe could stop them, his preferred attitude of levity briefly overcoming his predicament. "It's quite a mouthful, a bit like my c—"

Jayne's hand shot in the air so fast she almost sliced off an ear. "Mr Fox-Whittingham," she spat out, almost tripping over her words. "A woman has died. You were the last to see her alive. I suggest you start taking stock of what's going on here and act accordingly."

Rupe inwardly grinned. "Oh, I know exactly where I am, darling, but sitting here cursing my bad luck is going to achieve diddly-squat. I like to keep things light, fun."

"I'm not here to have fun," Jayne said stiffly. "I'm here to do my job."

Oh, this is going to be fun. She was wound as tight as a rubber band stretched to its limit. When the band snapped, he wanted to be right there, up close against that rather fine body of hers so he could feel the sharp snap against his skin. *Pleasure and pain.*

He pushed his chair away from the table and let his legs sprawl. He didn't miss the brief flick of her eyes to his groin. "Well then, *Ms* Seymour. Let's see how quickly you can get me out of here and into my bed."

THE DETECTIVE IN charge of questioning him sat opposite, a look of condemnation and resentment in his eyes. Ah, so that was his beef. Detective Fisher didn't like rich people. Rupe was willing to guess the detective despised what he saw as easy-to-come-by wealth. *Sanctimonious prick.* Rupe had worked his bollocks off for his money. It was hardly his fault he'd started a company that developed computer games that the world seemed to hanker after. He hadn't come from money. Rupe's dad had been a copper back in the day. That was how Rupe had first met Cash—his dad had been transferred from the Met to Northern Ireland when Rupe was eleven. Rupe knew more about the inner workings of a copper's mind than he'd let on to this Fisher dick.

Fisher set the tape and introduced everyone in the room.

"Can I get you anything before we start? A glass of water?"

Rupe shook his head.

"Okay, Mr Whittingham. Firstly, thank you for coming in to the police station to help us with our enquiries. I would like to reiterate that you are not under arrest. We just need to ascertain a few facts concerning the death of Mrs Vanessa Reynolds. Let's start with how you knew Mrs Reynolds."

Rupe kept his body loose. "No, let's start with you getting my name right. It's Mr *Fox*-Whittingham," he said, feeling a twinge of annoyance.

Fisher gave a wry smirk with no hint of embarrassment. "Of course. Mr Fox-Whittingham." He briefly nodded his head. "How did you first meet Mrs Reynolds?"

Rupe repressed a sigh. "Like I told you in the statement I gave yesterday, I come to London every few weeks on business. I met her in a club I like to spend a bit of time at when I'm over here."

Fisher perused his notes. "The Vault, correct?"

"Yeah."

"And was it you who first approached Mrs Reynolds, or the

other way around?"

"She approached me."

"And when was this, exactly?"

Despite the fact that Rupe had already given all the information the previous day, he kept his voice even. Jayne had warned him there would be a lot of repetition and that they'd ask him the same questions over and over to try to trip him up. Lies were harder to maintain than the truth.

"I don't remember the specific date. A year, give or take."

"And you began a relationship on that day?"

"I wouldn't say we had a relationship."

"Well, what would you say, exactly?" Fisher asked.

Rupe crossed his arms and narrowed his eyes. "I guess you could say we had a mutually beneficial arrangement. Or to put it another way, we were fuck buddies."

Fisher kept up the calm facade, but it was hard to miss the tightening of the skin around his eyes. Rupe glanced sideways at Jayne. She had her head bent, taking detailed notes in neat, precise handwriting. He willed her to look at him. She didn't.

"Okay," Fisher said. "Let's go back to that night. Tell me in your own words what happened."

Rupe couldn't repress his sigh this time. The repetition was getting on his one remaining nerve. Still, he had no option but to play their silly games.

"Nessa met me at the club and—"

"Nessa?" Fisher interjected even though he knew full well who Rupe was talking about.

Rupe set his jaw before something inadvisable spilled out. "Yeah, Nessa. Vanessa. Mrs Reynolds to you."

Fisher smirked and indicated for him to continue.

"I met her at the club. We had a few drinks, then a few more. I vaguely recall her asking me to come back to her hotel room. The next thing I remember is waking up, and Nessa had gone."

"Gone?"

Oh, this prick is really testing my limits now.

"Dead." Rupe held back a wince. "She was dead."

"And what are your theories on how a seemingly healthy young woman passed, Mr Fox-Whittingham?"

Was this dick for real? Rupe slowly grinned. "What can I say? I'm that fucking good in the sack."

Jayne touched his arm. It was meant as a warning, but a bolt of electricity shot up the limb and damn near stopped his heart.

Fisher leaned back, ignoring Rupe's interjection. "Let's go back to the club. Did you buy Mrs Reynolds's drinks?"

"Yeah."

"And what was she drinking?"

"Vodka, mainly. And a few shots."

A knock at the door cut off Fisher's next question, and a woman police officer entered. Fisher spoke for the tape and then motioned her over. She whispered something in his ear, and he nodded.

"Interview suspended at"—he looked at his watch—"eleven fifteen p.m."

"What's going on?" Rupe said. "Are we done?"

Fisher's mouth twisted in an attempt at a smile. "Not quite yet. I'll be back as soon as I can."

Fisher left the room, followed by his sidekick, who hadn't spoken but also hadn't taken his eyes off Rupe during the entire interview.

Rupe turned to Jayne. "Why would they cut the interview?"

Jayne finished scribbling on her pad before setting it on the table. She twisted in her seat and scowled at him. "What the hell are you playing at? Just answer their questions straight. No more stupid comments about being good in bed."

Rupe grinned at the disdain in her tone. "He was pissing me off."

She raised her eyes heavenward. "Did you listen to a thing I said earlier? I told you how he'd try to needle you, to get a rise.

Stay calm. Answer the questions fully, and then we can all get to bed."

"Now you're talking," Rupe said with an exaggerated wink.

Jayne blinked and shook her head. God, he already loved it when she reprimanded him, verbally or silently. When he got out of this shithole, he would make bedding Jayne Seymour his number-one priority. She was clearly a woman who liked the finer things in life—from her crisp designer suit to the Louboutins gracing her petite feet and the Mulberry handbag nestled by the table leg. Well, she'd come to the right place for that, and the fact that she was giving off "don't come anywhere near me, dickhead" vibes had his hunting instincts on high alert.

The door opened, and Fisher entered the interview room. "Sorry about that. Thanks for coming in, Mr Fox-Whittingham. You're free to go, but if I could ask you to remain in the country until this business is cleared up, just in case we have any more questions."

Rupe looked at the detective, then at Jayne, then back at Fisher again. "That's it?"

"For now, yes. We'll be in touch if we need anything further."

And with that, the coppers left him alone with Jayne. She gathered her papers together and slotted them into her bag.

"What the hell was all that about?" Rupe said, his normally lighthearted demeanour deserting him. "I missed the fucking rugby for this shit."

Jayne stood and slung her bag over her left shoulder. "The police are doing their jobs, Mr Fox-Whittingham." She sighed and then added in a patient tone, as though talking to a child, "As I have already explained, a woman has died. You were the last to see her alive. They want to follow up all leads, ensure no stone is left unturned. It's just routine." She tossed a business card onto the table. "If they call again, ring me before you say anything. Do *not* talk to them alone."

And with that, she swept out of the room.

5

Jayne's legs faltered as she staggered through her apartment door. Her eyes were stinging, both from lack of sleep and from the lateness of the hour. Added to her discomfort were the spasms that kept shooting up her spine, no doubt made worse by that awful metal chair in the police interview room.

She dropped her bag by the door and kicked her shoes off, letting them thud against the wall. Then she walked over to the thick rug that separated her living space from the open-plan kitchen. She curled her toes into the soft fibres, her feet aching like an absolute bitch.

The clock in the kitchen caught her eye. One fifteen. She had to be up at six. Life sucked sometimes, and she potentially had yet another case on her plate unless Darren kept to his word and took over. Although, with any luck, the police would drop any suspicions against her client, and she could file him away under "no further action required."

As her mind turned to her *client*, her skin prickled with irritation. *Arrogant little bastard.* She might have put his considerable ego down to his wealth, but over the years, she'd come across cocky sods without two pennies to rub together. In her experience, overconfidence rarely had anything to do with the size of a person's bank balance.

Rupert Fox-Whittingham. Even his name annoyed her. And when he'd made that almost-comment about the size of his penis... what a cock.

She chuckled at her own joke as she wandered to the fridge. Greeted with virtually bare shelves, she took out a pasta salad that was two days beyond its expiration date. Figuring that eating the salad wouldn't kill her, she peeled off the cellophane wrapper and tossed the packaging into the bin. In five minutes flat, she'd emptied the plastic container. Still feeling unsatisfied, she took a litre of ice cream from the fridge and began to eat it straight out of the carton. *Mmm, peanut butter.* Her favourite. Her hips and belly would disagree, but as she'd barely eaten in three days, she figured she'd earned a few high-calorie spoonfuls.

Halfway through the carton, she caught hold of herself and replaced the lid. Eating a whole litre of ice cream wouldn't make her feel better. Instead, she'd probably be up all night with a stomach ache. She put the dirty spoon and fork in the dishwasher and headed off to bed.

As she burrowed beneath the covers, a soft sigh escaped her. There wasn't much that could beat clean sheets and a bed she could spread out in. Her untidy sleeping style had been a source of consternation between her and Kyle for years. He'd been a very neat sleeper. He went to bed and woke up in the same position, the covers barely moving in the night. Her side of the bed, on the other hand, looked as though a tornado had blown through while they'd been sleeping.

Not that she needed to worry about that any more. Kyle's sleeping habits were no longer her concern.

A twinge of regret pinched at her insides. She closed her eyes and willed her brain to switch off. One of the negatives of getting home so late was the lack of affordability on the downtime stakes.

She'd barely get four and a half hours' kip, even if she fell straight to sleep—which she wouldn't.

Jayne was still staring at the green digital display of her alarm clock at two thirty in the morning without having managed one minute of unconsciousness. She shoved the covers to one side and padded into the kitchen to make a cup of warm milk.

She set the pan on the stove and poured in the milk before turning the gas to a low heat. While it was warming up, she wandered into the living room and stared out of the window. The full moon cast a shimmering glow across the Thames, the water as still as a millpond.

As the sound of hissing milk reached her, she crossed the living room and turned off the gas. After pouring the bubbling liquid into a cup, she blew across the top and took a sip. *Needs sugar.* She added three heaped spoonfuls and took another sip. *Better.*

She set the steaming drink on a coaster on her bedside table and slipped beneath the covers once more. Perhaps a few minutes of reading combined with the milk would do the trick. She opened her bedside drawer and took out her current book, a novel she'd started weeks ago. She was still only on chapter four. It wasn't that she didn't like reading. In fact, immersing herself in a story far from her own life soothed her. It was simply a matter of time—or rather the lack of it.

As her eyes scanned the typeface, her lids slowly began to droop. The book fell into her lap, and she felt herself drifting through that heavenly moment between consciousness and slumber.

And then her damn phone dinged with a text.

Her eyes snapped open. If that was Kyle, she would cut his goddamn balls off. Metaphorically, of course. Unfortunately, grievous bodily harm to one's cheating ex wasn't acceptable in civilised society. *More's the pity.*

She lifted her phone. The text was from a mobile but not a number she recognised.

With a frown, she read the message: *How about dinner tomorrow night?*

It was signed "RFW."

Her immediate thought was, *Are you fucking kidding me?*

And... it didn't stay a thought. She stabbed out those five words into her phone and hit Send.

His reply came straight back:

Aww, come on, Jayne. I'll make sure you have fun. Go on, change the habit of a lifetime and let your hair down.

He'd even added a winking emoji at the end.

Jayne decided that engaging in a tit-for-tat texting session wouldn't get her anywhere. Instead, she turned down the volume on her phone, set it upside down so the light going off wouldn't disturb her, and buried her head under the covers.

She was vaguely aware of a couple more texts arriving—which she studiously ignored—but at last sleep claimed her.

The following morning, she arrived at the office before seven thirty. It would be an hour or so before Donna arrived, so she started the coffee percolator, which her absolute gem of a PA had already prepared the previous day for a straight switch-on.

She sank into her chair. Another rammed day loomed ahead. She needed a holiday—some downtime. Sand, sun, and a never-ending supply of mojitos sounded like... an impossible dream, given her caseload. Right then, she vowed that as soon as the three imminent cases she was working on were over, she'd take a break. She could at least fit in a long weekend in Barcelona, a city that had everything: culture, great food, and a damn fine beach.

The rest of the morning passed in a blur. Donna had left a gap in Jayne's diary to allow her to grab some lunch. *God bless that woman.* Her PA would happily grab her a bite to eat, but Jayne preferred to get her own. The fifteen minutes standing in a queue at the deli was often the only break she got.

As Jayne rose from her chair to go and get a sandwich, a light tap sounded at her door.

"Come in," she called out.

Donna poked her head into Jayne's office. "I know you're probably going to lunch soon, but you have a visitor."

Jayne mouthed, "Not Kyle?"

Donna shook her head, but before she could explain who the visitor was, the office door eased wide-open, and standing there with a foppish grin to rival Hugh Grant was Rupert Fox-Whittingham.

"Sorry to disturb," he said, his expression the direct opposite of his apologetic words. He flashed Donna a full-on white-toothed smile. "Thanks, darling. You're a dream."

Donna blushed and coyly dipped her head. Jayne repressed a groan. Her PA wasn't a blusher. Damn Rupert Fox-Whittingham and his plum-in-the-mouth charm. Donna gave Jayne a contrite smile as Rupert sauntered into her office and made himself at home on her couch.

As the door closed with a quiet click, Rupert crossed his legs, spread his right arm over the back of her sofa, and patted the spare seat beside him. "Come and sit with me, Jayne."

She ignored his invitation, choosing instead to sit back behind her desk. "What are you doing here, Mr Fox-Whittingham?"

"You didn't answer my texts."

"No, that's right. I didn't. And normally, when one is ignored, one gets the hint."

He grinned at her, the smile slowly reaching his warm chocolate eyes and making them sparkle like diamonds set against a velvet backdrop. She turned away. She didn't want to notice his eyes. She had sworn off men, and this posh git wasn't about to change that, especially as he was a client.

"And because you didn't answer, you gave me no choice but to turn up here at your—may I say—*delightful* offices to extend my invitation to dinner in person."

Jayne held back a laugh. The man was a walking, talking throwback to the fifties.

"Well, I'm sorry you had a wasted journey," Jayne said, pointing her pen at the door. "Now, if you don't mind, I have a very busy afternoon."

That smile came at her again, slowly inching its way into her psyche. She turned away and began to write utter rubbish on her pad. Doodles, random words, anything to avoid those come-to-bed eyes and inviting smile.

A slight rustle reached her ears, but she refused to look up—until the damn man perched his left buttock on the corner of her desk. The corner right beside her.

She held her body still. Only her head moved. She fixed him with the disdainful stare usually reserved for Kyle. "What do you think you are doing?"

"Moving closer." He bent his head until his nose was about an inch from her hair. He closed his eyes and took a deep breath. "You smell of summer, Jayne. Intoxicating."

A fluttering set off in her abdomen. Oh no, this was *not* happening. She needed this man out of her office. *Right now.*

She pushed back her chair and got to her feet. Avoiding his end of the desk, she strode across to the other side of her office and opened the door. "As I said, Mr Fox-Whittingham, I'm busy. I'm very glad that I could be of service to you yesterday, but as our business is concluded, I would like you to leave."

Rupert ambled towards her, his gait that of a man who was uberconfident and usually got what he wanted. *Well, isn't disappointment a bitch.*

As he reached her, he paused. "Just one dinner. How bad could it be?"

"I don't go on dinner dates with my clients."

"You just said our business was concluded."

"Or ex-clients. Goodbye, Mr Fox-Whittingham."

He leaned forward, and his breath caressed the shell of her ear as he whispered, "I'm starting to like it when you call me that."

And with a final quick wink, he left.

6

Rupe closed the door behind him, still wearing the smile he'd had in Jayne's office. Christ, that frosty exterior was going to be fun to melt. He wasn't put off in the slightest by her summary dismissal. In fact, the challenge she posed made him more excited than he'd felt in a long time. With his wealth, success with women came easily. The difficulty was finding a woman who intrigued, who put fire in his belly, and who, with a simple haughty stare, pumped enough blood to his cock to keep him stiff all day.

And more than that, despite her frostiness, he liked her.

Outside Jayne's office, he flagged down a passing black cab and gave his home address. The traffic was light, so he arrived home in fifteen minutes. As he entered through the front door, his phone rang. A spike of hope that it might be Jayne zinged through his gut. He took his phone out of his pocket. Unfortunately, optimism was replaced with reality.

"Thanks for the update." Cash's irritated voice almost sliced through his eardrum.

Rupe nudged the front door closed. "Sorry, bud. I've been a bit distracted."

"I had to call the fucking station and put up with some condescending prick telling me they'd finished their questioning last night and let you go."

"Yeah. Sorry. I'm still a bit all over the place."

"So that's it?" Cash said.

"I'm hoping so."

"What did your lawyer say?"

A delicious shiver vibrated down Rupe's spine. "Not much. Just if they pulled me in again to call her."

"That's good advice. Follow it."

Oh, I'll be following it all right.

"Are you going to make it over to see us before you go back to the Caribbean?" Cash asked.

"The police want me to stick around until this business with Nessa is sorted out." That fact had irritated him at first, but now he quite liked the excuse of having to remain in London. It meant he could work on defrosting Jayne without awkward questions from Cash, who knew him too well. Rupe rarely spent more than a week at a time in London. "So, yeah, I'll pop across in the next couple of days."

"Okay, great. Stay in touch, dickhead."

He smiled as Cash cut the call. He might not see as much of his friend as he used to since Cash and Tally had moved out of London—they preferred the countryside of Gloucestershire to bring up their kids—but they were always there if he needed them.

He fetched his laptop from his study and took it through to the kitchen. After putting a pot of coffee on, he began researching Ms Jayne Seymour. If he had any chance of persuading her to come to dinner, he needed an angle. In his experience, women only gave off such strong signals for men to keep away when they'd been badly hurt.

Time to find out how Jayne had got her scars.

~

As Jayne turned up for work on Friday, she made two promises to herself: one, she wasn't working past six that night, and two, she was going to leave all her casework in the office and take the entire weekend off. She'd go to see Ganny, maybe stay over. And then, on Sunday, she could take the bus down to the coast. The sea air would regenerate her depleted batteries as it always did. She had to do something. She recognised the signs of burnout all too well.

Jayne waved at the night guard as she acknowledged to herself that she rarely saw daytime security. She usually arrived before their shift began and left after it had ended—another reason to keep promise number two.

The lift doors opened at her floor, and she juggled her laptop, her bag full of files, her handbag, and her keys. When getting the key in the lock proved to be a struggle, she dropped her bags on the floor, making the job of opening up much easier.

As she nudged at the door, the first thing that hit her was the smell. Her nostrils filled with the sweet scent of flowers. Pushing the door wide, she froze. Her office was full of white and pink roses. A bouquet sat on top of every available surface, including the narrow window ledge.

Leaving her bags outside, Jane edged farther into the room. She wandered around, touching the odd petal, the silkiness pleasant beneath her fingers. She looked for a card but couldn't see one.

"Wow, did someone mistake your office for a florist's?"

Jayne turned to find Donna leaning against the doorframe, an expression of amazement on her face.

Jayne narrowed her eyes. "Do you know anything about this? How did they get in here?"

Donna shook her head. "No idea. It's pretty cool, though. You've clearly got an admirer." She stepped over the threshold and stuck her nose into the nearest bouquet, sniffing deeply. "And one with a few bob to spare."

As Donna said that, a realisation hit Jayne. *Of course.* This was just the sort of over-the-top gesture someone as rich as Rupert Fox-Whittingham would go for. She ground her teeth and let out a deep breath through her nose. Stepping behind her desk, she noticed a couple of bouquets in their own individual water pockets. Jayne moved them to one side and found an envelope with her name scrawled on the front in black ink.

She stuck her nail into the flap, opened it, and pulled out the note:

"Roses remind me of you, Jayne. Sweet scented, beautiful, intriguing. But get too close, and those thorns will tear through flesh with ease."

The note had no signature, but it wasn't necessary. That message was all the confirmation she needed. With her annoyance increasing to full-on anger, she scooped the bouquets off her desk and dumped them on the floor.

"Donna," she said, her tone clipped and businesslike, making her PA stand up straight and replace the look of awe with a more professional expression. "Arrange to have these flowers taken to the nearest old people's home, would you? And then cancel my morning appointments."

∽

IT HADN'T TAKEN Jayne very long to find out where Rupert Fox-Whittingham laid his head at night. As the taxi pulled up outside the large country-style house covered in ivy and—*goddammit*—roses over the door, her stomach twisted with annoyance. The problem with moneyed guys who also happened to be good-looking was that they thought they could have anything they wanted.

Well, she was there to tell Mr Fox-Whittingham once and for all that she wasn't for sale. At any price.

As she walked to the front door, her heels sank into the gravel. Stupid, pretentious driveway. *What's wrong with good old-fashioned tarmac? Or paving flags?* The only thing worse than gravel for a woman wearing heels was cobbles. Both must have been created by men who wanted to have a chuckle at women's expense.

The strap on her bag fell down her arm as she reached up to rap on the door. She reset it on her shoulder and knocked a couple of times.

When the door opened, her mouth was already open, ready to give him a piece of her mind. The sight of a woman in her midforties standing in the hallway made it snap shut. Her dark hair was fashioned into a bun, wisps skimming her cheeks where they'd managed to break free from the many bobby pins.

"Hi," the woman said in a friendly tone as she rubbed her flour-covered hands down her apron.

Jayne rocked back on her heels. "Sorry to disturb you. I'm looking for Rupert Fox-Whittingham. I must have the wrong house."

"No, no, dear. You're at the right place. I'm his housekeeper. Please do come in." She stepped back from the doorstep and gestured for her to enter.

"Oh, I can't stay. I just need a quick word."

"Nonsense," she said. "No need to stand on the front step when there's a house full of rooms. Plus, I need a female opinion on the chocolate cake I made earlier."

And with that, leaving the front door wide open with Jayne hovering at the entrance, Rupert's housekeeper turned on her heel and disappeared down the hallway.

Jayne expelled a sigh. This was not going to plan. She stepped inside the house and shut the door behind her. With her heels clacking on the stone floor, she followed in the direction she thought the housekeeper had gone. The generous hallway had several rooms to the left and right with their doors closed. Jayne followed her nose and found herself inside a large farmhouse-style kitchen—all oak cupboards and wooden tops, oiled to perfection. In the centre of the room was a huge island with chairs nestled beneath and various stainless-steel pans hanging overhead.

"I'm Abi." The housekeeper placed a three-tiered chocolate cake on the centre island. She took out a large knife from a wooden block on the countertop and sliced into the cake. "You must be Jayne."

Jayne tilted her head in surprise. "How do you know my name?"

Abi waved her hand dismissively before sticking a large triangular piece of chocolate cake on a plate and pushing it across to Jayne. "Rupert told me. He saw you getting out of the cab, asked me to let you in, and then disappeared off somewhere. He'll be back shortly, no doubt."

Jayne stiffened. She stared down at her hands and found she was clenching and unclenching them. He was *unbelievable*. He'd guessed why she'd come and used a stupid tactic to get her inside his house. Her face heated as anger flushed through her system.

"I'll bet he did," she muttered under her breath, and then said in a louder voice, "I can't stay, unfortunately. Work and all that. I'll text him."

As she turned around, she came face-to-face with Rupert. He was standing with his arms braced on either side of the door to the kitchen, his white long-sleeved shirt stretched across the tight, flat muscles of his chest. *Not looking at his chest. Nope. Nothing to see there.* She dragged her gaze to his face. The damned man was laughing at her.

"Leaving already, Jayne? Surely not before we've had chance to chat."

She crossed the kitchen and stood right in front of him. "I came by to tell you that the local old people's home very much appreciates your kind gift. Oh, and to say that if you keep harassing me, or break into my office again, waking up next to a dead woman will be the least of your problems."

Rupert's lips curved into a smirk. "See, I was right about the thorns. Thing is, Jayne, I have a very high pain threshold. A few scratches here and there aren't likely to damage me."

"Probably not," she said, forcing her lips into a smile that no doubt looked more like a grimace. "But a knee to the balls will. So hear me loud and clear. I'm. Not. Interested. Got it?"

Rupert threw back his head and laughed. "You are enchanting. Fascinating. Come on. One dinner. That's all I ask. And if, by the end of the night, the thought of me still makes your skin crawl, I'll back away, and you'll never have to see me again."

Jayne rubbed her fingers over her lips as she considered the offer from the annoying-as-hell man who stood before her, his arms still barring her exit. His actions so far told her he wasn't simply going to disappear or leave her in peace, and while she could get rid of him legally by slapping a restraining order on him, she didn't want to do that. He didn't deserve such harsh treatment, and in the unlikely event the police did come sniffing around again, asking more questions about the death of Vanessa Reynolds, it wouldn't look good if his own lawyer had taken out a restraining order. He was as annoying as a fly buzzing round her head, though. If only she could swat him away so easily. Or squirt him with a good dose of Raid.

"Fine," she said, drawing a winning smile from Rupert. "One dinner. Tonight, or never. And I want to eat at The Berkeley."

She added the latter with a wicked smile. Getting a table at The Berkeley at such short notice would be nigh on impossible, which would mean she'd be able to legitimately renege on the deal. At least trying to secure a booking would give him something to do for the rest of the day.

"Perfect," he said, not even remotely thrown by her set of

demands. "Marcus Wareing is a dear friend. I'm sure he'll sort me out. I'll pick you up at seven thirty."

Jayne inwardly cursed. Marcus Wareing was the owner of the Michelin-starred restaurant at The Berkeley. She'd thrown down an impossible challenge only to find that the man standing in front of her was more than up to the task. With an irritated huff, she brushed past him and walked outside, feeling manipulated and backed into a corner.

Still, it was one dinner. She might manage that without killing him.

7

Rupe stood outside Jayne's apartment and raised his hand. Rather than knocking, however, he let his hand fall back to his side and took a couple of deep breaths to compose himself. Up until that point, he'd been his usual flippant self around her. That strategy was a mistake with someone like Jayne Seymour. It was time to change his plan of attack.

During his research, he'd discovered she was going through a divorce. Her husband seemed a bit of a dick, a waster, and definitely not worthy of a classy lady like Jayne. Rupe wondered what the story was—why she'd ended up with someone like Kyle Thomas and the reason for the split. Instinct told him she'd been hurt and that was why she was draped in enough man repellent to put off the keenest of hopefuls.

The bad news for Jayne was that Rupe had a hide like a rhinoceros when it came to insults. They simply bounced off him. Just as well, because Jayne's aim was as good as an Olympic javelin champion.

He also knew why she'd insisted on going to dinner that night and thrown what she thought was a curveball with the whole *Berkeley* demand. She hadn't wanted to agree to a dinner at all, but her inherent good manners had won out, so she'd drawn on her experience of negotiation and thrown down a difficult challenge. It was a shame for her that his contacts and influence stretched far and wide. In fact, it wouldn't have mattered which restaurant she'd picked. Either he or Cash would have been able to swing a table in a matter of a few phone calls.

Enough with the procrastinating. He lifted his clenched fist and rapped on the door. After a few moments, he heard chains rattling and the key turning in the lock. As Jayne opened the door, he caught his breath. He'd half expected her to dress down as a way of needling him. She hadn't.

Jayne had chosen an emerald-green dress, knee length and off the shoulder. The colour was a perfect complement to her soft hazel eyes. The dress clung to every single curve—the promise of what lay beneath going off in his head like fireworks on Bonfire Night. On her feet, a pair of silver open-toed slingbacks added at least four inches to her height, bringing her virtually eye-to-eye with him. Her blond hair lay in loose waves over her shoulders. It was longer than he'd thought, but considering that every time he'd seen her she'd worn it up, he wouldn't have known the length. Her makeup was light, apart from a bright-red glossy lipstick that decorated those amazing lips.

"Wow," he said. "You look stunning. No, strike that. You *are* stunning."

He half expected a witty comeback. Instead, she gave him a proper ice-free smile that made his stomach clench and his cock twitch.

"You don't scrub up too badly yourself, Mr Fox-Whittingham," she said.

"Oh God," Rupe replied with a groan. "You're going to call me that all night, aren't you?"

She laughed. *Oh, that sound.* He'd flay himself if it meant he could hear it again.

"Okay, let's go with *Rupert* for tonight only. You're still technically my client."

"Well, seeing as you're in an amiable mood, can we go with Rupe? My mother was the only one to regularly call me Rupert, and usually only when I'd been very, very bad."

Jayne frowned. "Was?"

"Yeah," Rupe said, biting down on the surge of grief that rose within him. "She died. Eighteen months ago. Cancer."

"I'm so sorry." Jayne sounded genuinely sympathetic.

Rupe shook his head. "Let's not start our evening on a maudlin note. I'm trying to persuade you this shouldn't be a one-night deal."

Jayne raised an eyebrow. "I hope you got in at The Berkeley."

"What the lady demands," he said, sticking out his elbow. He couldn't hold back his smile when Jayne slipped her hand through. He did, however, manage to repress a hiss as that same jolt of electricity he'd experienced at the police station—the last time she touched him—shot up his arm. This woman might well be the death of him—literally.

His driver was waiting a short distance away from Jayne's apartment. Rupe guided her into the back of the car, and once the door had closed, the noise from the street abated.

"We could have taken a taxi," Jayne said, nodding towards the front of the car, which Rupe had sealed with a privacy screen.

"Why would I do that? The equivalent would be renting a place to live when you already have a perfectly good house in the right location that's paid for."

She peered at him through a narrowed gaze. "You really are filthy rich, aren't you?"

Rupe flashed her a winning smile. "Oh, I'm very filthy, darling. Rich is just one of the terms to tag onto the end of that adjective."

Jayne raised her eyes heavenward. "You're an impossible cad, Rupert Fox-Whittingham."

Rupe chuckled. "My best friend's missus always says that."

"Is that the same friend who called my partner to see if we could take on your case?"

"The very same." Rupe tilted his head to one side. "I take it you're not a tennis fan?"

"Sport? I barely get time to eat, let alone any me time."

"Cash used to be the number-one tennis player in the world."

"That's impressive."

"Yeah. He retired four years ago. He could have still been playing today, but, well, he met Tally, had a couple of kids, and decided family was more important than tennis."

"Lucky them." A tinge of envy coloured her tone. "Glad it works out for some people."

Rupe kept his face straight. Her offhand comment told him that his assumptions were correct. She'd been hurt and had probably sworn off men as a result. He didn't respond, sensing that it wasn't the right time to probe. After a glass or two of Prosecco, he'd test the waters.

"So why did you choose The Berkeley?" he asked, even though he knew the answer.

Her smile was as fleeting as the hint of devilment in her eyes, but he spotted both. "Because I thought you wouldn't be able to pull it off at such short notice."

Rupe clasped a hand to his chest and pasted a faux-aggrieved look on his face. "I'm hurt you would do such a thing."

Jayne squinted at him. "I get the feeling I'd have to work a damn sight harder to really offend you."

Rupe chuckled. Jayne would be a tough nut to crack, but hell, he was going to have a ball trying.

His car pulled to a stop, and Rupe looked out of the window. "Great, we're here." He jumped out and went around to Jayne's side, but he should have known better. She was already out of the car and standing on the pavement, her clutch bag clenched between her fingers.

He waggled his finger in admonishment. "I'm an old-fashioned kind of guy."

Jayne pointed to herself. "Millennial. Independent and proud."

Rupe threw his head back and laughed. "You can get the door, then," he said, waving at the entrance to the hotel.

Jayne walked ahead, which gave Rupe the chance to check out her arse. Not that it was the first time he had, but a sight like that never got boring. Her hips swayed as she moved—a hint of sexiness without being overt. Jayne was a serious girl, which was why he'd have to rein in the "Rupert-ness." Blatant attempts at seduction or crude overtures would see him eating alone.

As he'd requested, their table was situated in a secluded part of the restaurant. Once seated, the waiter handed over their menus and left them alone.

"Would you like red or white wine with dinner, or shall I order both?" Rupe asked, his head buried in the wine list.

"Neither," Jayne replied, causing him to lift his head. "I'll stick to water, thanks."

So much for my plan to get her tipsy. He raised an eyebrow. "You don't drink?"

"You say that like it's a crime. Yes, I drink. When I've had a bad day at work, or if I'm out with friends, I might have a glass or two of wine."

Rupe gave her a wry smile. "Message received. At least I'll know I've made it into the Jayne Seymour inner circle when you let me buy you a drink."

"It's an exclusive club. I doubt you'll gain entry."

"I like a challenge."

Jayne leaned back in her chair and folded her arms across her chest. Her gaze was unwavering as she locked onto his. "If I had to guess, I'd say you have an extremely low boredom threshold and I'm not interesting enough to hold your attention. Work is my life, which doesn't leave me time for anything else. I think you'll discover my limitations this evening, and I won't need to worry about you mithering me for another date, which would be a good result for both of us."

Rupe found himself unable to look away from those hazel eyes that held so much mystery and secretiveness. The words Jayne had used betrayed an underlying lack of self-esteem that wasn't obvious at first glance. He wondered if her confidence had always been low or if the marriage breakdown had contributed to that. He'd bet on the latter. A successful lawyer wouldn't usually be lacking in confidence.

"You're right. I do get bored easily." He leaned forward and lowered his voice. "But there's something about you. I can't put my finger on it. You intrigue me."

Before she could respond, Rupe gestured to the waiter and ordered their drinks: a bottle of red for him and a mineral water for her.

"So what are you going to order?" He rubbed his chin. "I'd guess you're a fish or chicken kind of woman."

Jayne's mouth creased in thought. "Why would you say that?"

Rupe swept his gaze lazily over her, and on its trip back up to her face, he lingered on her breasts. "You don't get to keep a figure like yours while stuffing your face with hunks of beef."

"Depends on the hunk of beef," she hit back with a twinkle in those stunning eyes.

Rupe raised one eyebrow. "Was that a sexual innuendo?"

Jayne laughed, making Rupe's skin tingle deliciously.

"I'm not sure you're good for me, Rupert Fox-Whittingham."

Rupe grinned. "Bad is way more fun, Jayne."

After they'd eaten, Rupe ordered coffee. Just watching Jayne blow delicately across the top of the steaming cup made his stomach tighten.

"I expected you to give me a tough time tonight," Rupe said, taking a couple of sips of his own drink.

Jayne cocked her head to one side. "It crossed my mind. I

considered several approaches, from monosyllabic to acerbic, especially as you manipulated me into coming." Jayne let out a soft sigh, which made Rupe chuckle. "And then I decided I'm just too damned tired to be combative tonight."

"Heavy workload?"

"Yeah. I keep promising I'll take a break, and then more work lands on my desk."

"Like hapless billionaires needing an extraction from a tricky situation," Rupe said.

Jayne chuckled. "Exactly like that. I'm taking this weekend off, though. Going to see my grandmother."

Rupe leaned back in his chair. His research had told him Jayne's parents were dead and her grandmother was her only living family. She had no siblings and was in the middle of a messy divorce. No wonder she worked all the time.

"You should take a longer period of time off. It's important to be kind to yourself."

Jayne's face softened, and a surge of desire mixed with hope raced through Rupe's body. Maybe he was breaking down some barriers.

"So tell me," he said in an effort to distract himself from the growing bulge in his trousers. "Who hurt you so badly that you felt the need to become the ice queen? Because from what I've seen tonight, there's definitely molten lava beneath the surface."

Jayne dropped her cup with a clang. Coffee spilled down the sides and gathered in a pool in the saucer. "Who said anyone hurt me?"

"I did—and you did with that reaction." He nodded at her cup.

Jayne shook her head. She pushed back her chair and gracefully got to her feet.

"Thank you, Rupert. You've just made a decision for me." And with that, she picked up her clutch bag, spun on her heel, and headed for the exit.

"Shit." Rupe scrambled to his feet. There was no time to wait for the bill, so he threw a more than generous bundle of notes on the table and set off after Jayne.

She was already way ahead of him. Those long legs of hers easily ate up the yards.

He caught up with her outside the restaurant. "I'm sorry," he said, clasping her elbow. "I shouldn't have pried."

Jayne stepped away, causing his hand to fall to his side. "I kept my end of the bargain. Against my principles and better judgement, I went to dinner with you. Now, kindly leave me be."

She put her hand in the air, but when two cabs passed by without stopping, she let her arm fall to her side, an irritated sigh spilling from her lips. She craned her neck, looking up the street, getting ready to hail the next one she saw.

"Let me see you home. You could be waiting ages for a cab."

Her eyes cut to his. He watched in silence as she weighed her options. She could stand there hoping to eventually get lucky and grab a taxi, or she could take a ride home with him. Reading the disdainful expression on her face, he hazarded a guess that she'd rather take a ride home with a piranha.

Rupe didn't wait for a reply. He called for his car, and thirty seconds later, it stopped by the side of the road. Rupe opened the back door.

"Come on, Jayne. Get in."

A couple of seconds scraped by, and then, without saying a word, she climbed inside. With a sigh of relief, Rupe got in beside her. Jayne had her back to him, giving him the cold shoulder physically and metaphorically. He decided to leave her be. His questioning had clearly touched a very raw nerve, and he cursed himself for cocking up so spectacularly.

She still hadn't uttered a word when they stopped outside her apartment building twenty minutes later. She unclipped her seatbelt. "Goodnight, Rupert," she said in a curt tone.

The car door slammed behind her, and she disappeared

inside. Rupe hesitated for a couple of seconds. Then he muttered, "Fuck it," and ran in after her. He took off up the stairwell. It'd be quicker than waiting for the lift. When he reached her floor, a little out of breath, he paused for a few seconds before banging on her door.

"Jayne, open up."

Silence.

"Jayne, for fuck's sake. I'm sorry, okay? My timing was off. It's none of my business. Just let me in. Five minutes—that's all I ask."

More silence.

"Fine. I don't have anywhere to be. I'll just settle in here for the night."

Rupe slid down the wall and pulled his knees into his chest, wrapping his arms around them. *Stubborn bloody woman. What the hell am I doing here, huh?* He could pick out a dozen women who'd have been quite happy to entertain him for the night. The problem was, he didn't want a dozen women. He wanted one woman. Trust him to home in on the elusive, principled lawyer.

His head snapped up when the lock rattled. Jayne opened the door as Rupe scrambled to his feet.

"You're an idiot," she said as he dusted off his trousers.

He gave her a goofy grin. "Guilty as charged."

She turned around and left the door open. He followed her and closed it behind him. Jayne sat on the couch and curled her feet beneath her.

"If you must know," she said as he settled himself into a chair at right angles to the couch, "I caught my husband screwing my best friend over that table." She winced as she pointed to a large, rectangular dining table on the far side of the open-plan room. "He's being an arse over the divorce because he thinks he's owed more than I think he's owed." She gave him a look of surprise. "And I have no idea why I just told you all that."

Rupe stroked his chin. "What does he think he's owed?"

Jayne shrugged one shoulder. "Half of everything, despite putting very little financially into our marriage."

"Cheeky fucker."

Her mouth twitched at the corners. "That's one of the nicer terms I'd use to describe him."

Rupe leaned forward, his forearms resting on his thighs. "I'm sorry. That's a shitty hand to be dealt."

"Yeah, well." Jayne picked at a thread on her dress. "I only wasted seven years on the deadbeat."

Rupe tilted his head to the side. "Am I forgiven?"

She let out a resigned sigh. "Do you always get your own way?"

He chuckled. "Usually."

Jayne stood, and for a moment he thought she was signalling for him to go. Instead, she wandered into the kitchen and returned with a bottle of white wine and two glasses.

"Make yourself useful," she said, thrusting the bottle and a corkscrew at him.

He raised an eyebrow. "Wow. I expected to have to work a lot harder to make it onto the list."

"Oh, you haven't, but seeing as I can't seem to get rid of you, I'm going to need a drink to help me cope."

Rupe flashed her a winning smile as he uncorked the bottle and poured the wine. He handed one over to Jayne, and they clinked their glasses together.

"To inner circles," he said.

"And annoying, pompous rich guys," she replied.

8

Jayne began to relax as she sipped her wine and listened to Rupe talk about his business. Who would have thought there was so much money in computer games? Despite all his shortcomings, he'd grown on her. He was a terrible cad and a playboy for sure, but underneath all that, she sensed a pretty decent guy.

And he wasn't too bad on the eyes either.

She shook that thought away. She'd failed as a wife and as a woman. Her career was all she had left, and getting involved with a client went against her self-imposed ethics. Plus, who needed a man anyway?

"Want a top-up?" she said, nodding at his empty glass.

"Wow. A second glass? That must move me up the list surely?"

Jayne swiped the glass from his hand and poured them both refills. "Here. But that's your lot. And two glasses of wine do not get you an entrance ticket."

Rupe laughed and glanced at his watch. "It's way past my bedtime anyway. You're a terrible influence on me."

"You've definitely got that the wrong way around," Jayne said. A knock on the door interrupted her next thought. She frowned and then rolled her eyes. Only one person would be so self-absorbed as to assume that calling unannounced, when it was past eleven, was acceptable behaviour.

"Are you expecting someone?" A strange expression crossed Rupert's face. "Do you want me to go?"

"No, stay," Jayne said a little too quickly, causing Rupe scratch his cheek in confusion. "It'll be Kyle. My soon-to-be ex," she added by way of explanation.

His eyebrows shot up towards his hairline. "At this time?"

Jayne nodded as another knock came at the door, definitely sounding more irritated than the first one. "He doesn't believe in boundaries."

Rupe stood, his posture stiff. He crossed his arms over his chest. "Well, maybe I'll have to bloody well point them out."

Jayne patted his shoulder on the way to the door. "I appreciate the sentiment, but tone down the alpha, please. You'll only make things worse. Leave him to me."

Jayne drew to a halt in front of the door and took a deep breath. She pressed her eye to the peephole. *Yep. Kyle.* Red-faced. Just what she didn't need.

She opened the door. "What do you want, Kyle?" she said in a bored tone. "Do you have any idea what time it is?"

He brushed past her without being invited but came to a hard stop when he saw Rupe. He glanced over his shoulder at Jayne. "Well, well. No wonder it's inconvenient. Did I interrupt something, Jayne?"

Jayne shot a warning glare at Rupe as he began to speak. She put herself between the two men. "I'll ask again. What do you want, Kyle?"

Kyle planted his hands on his hips—a habit that always made Jayne chuckle because he looked so effeminate, which wasn't his intention at all.

"I got your latest offer."

"And?"

"It's a no, Jayne. You know what I want."

"Well, that's a shame, Kyle, because that's my best and final offer. The next one will be fifty per cent less, so I'd act quickly if I were you."

Jayne didn't need to see Rupe to know he was bristling behind her. She put a hand behind her back and stuck up her thumb in an attempt to convey that she was fine. Handling Kyle was something she'd become an expert at. It would only make the situation worse if Rupe tried to get involved.

Kyle made a scoffing noise. "You wouldn't dare."

Jayne laughed but made sure the sound was hollow, almost condescending. "If I chose to, I could tie you up in legal knots for years." It was completely untrue, but he wouldn't know that. He'd never taken an interest in her career. "Don't be a dick your whole life, Kyle. Accept the terms, I'll sign the divorce papers, and you and I can go our separate ways."

"You bitch." Kyle's hands closed around Jayne's upper arms, and he shook her so hard that her brain rattled inside her skull. Before she had a chance to react, she found herself free.

She blinked a couple of times. Rupe had Kyle on the ground, one arm twisted up his back and Rupe's knee digging right into Kyle's lower spine. Kyle grunted and tried to wriggle free. Rupe tightened his grip.

"Apologise to the lady," Rupe gritted out.

"Fuck you."

Rupe pushed Kyle's arm farther up his back. Kyle cried out in pain.

"Apologise, or I'll break your arm."

"Rupe, no," Jayne said, keeping her tone low and firm in an effort to calm the escalating tension. "It's what he wants. You'll get in trouble. Let him go."

Rupe met her gaze and nodded but then grabbed Kyle by his hair and slammed his face into the floor. Kyle howled as blood spurted from his nose all over her oak flooring.

"Goddammit," she said as Kyle staggered to his feet, clutching his face. "If that stains, Rupert Fox-Whittingham, you're paying for the cleanup."

Rupe burst out laughing. "Cheap at half the price."

"I'm going to press charges." Kyle lurched over to the door, blood oozing through his fingers.

"You do that, buddy." Rupe shoved him in the back. He slammed the door behind Kyle and turned to face her. "What a cock."

Jayne huffed in frustration. "I told you to leave it."

"He put his hands on you," Rupe said in an incredulous tone. "I'm not going to stand around and let him rough you up."

"Haven't you had enough of being questioned by the police?"

When Rupe remained silent, Jayne let out a sigh. "Kyle's a coward. He wouldn't have done anything. You should have let me handle it. All you've done is given him more leverage. He will sue, you know, especially when he finds out who you are."

Rupe shrugged. "Whatever."

Jayne swept a hand over her face. "Look, I'm tired. Let's call it a night."

Rupe rubbed the back of his neck. "Have I fucked this up?" he said, swinging his hand between the two of them.

"We don't have a *this*."

"Yet," Rupe said with a wolfish grin.

Despite her irritation, Jayne gave him the briefest of smiles before shoving him in the shoulder. "Go on. Out. I've got to clean Kyle's bodily fluids off my floor before I can get to bed, thanks to you."

"I'll help you."

Jayne raised her eyebrows. "When was the last time you scrubbed a floor?"

Rupe laughed. "Fair point. Can I see you tomorrow?"

Jayne shook her head. "I'm visiting my grandmother, remember?"

"Sorry. Of course. Next week, then."

"I've got a lot on at work."

"I'll call you."

"Fine," she said, drawing a triumphant look from Rupe. "Now, go."

After she'd closed the door, Jayne drifted over to the window. Rupe appeared outside her apartment building, and an uneasy feeling stirred inside her as she watched him climb into his car. This wasn't good. A funny, smart, good-looking guy who defended a girl's honour was the stuff dreams were made of. Except none of that mattered, because it couldn't go anywhere.

She baulked as she cleaned up Kyle's blood—the thick, gloopy fluid reminding her of spilled eggs when the liquid wouldn't absorb into the paper towel. Once her floor was blood-free, she cleared away the wine glasses and put the wine back in the fridge. As she entered her bedroom, the bed seemed to overwhelm the space, almost as though it were mocking her singleton status. Ridiculous really. She'd bought it when she'd thrown Kyle out, almost as a symbolic "screw you"—a super-king-sized bed for a woman who liked to sprawl and now could.

She changed for bed and flicked off the light, praying for a full night's sleep free of dreams.

~

Jayne woke, not to daylight streaming through her blinds but to the blaring of her phone. Her immediate thought was Ganny. She scrabbled about until her hand closed around it. Her heart thundered in her chest

"Hello," she said breathlessly.

"Jayne." Rupe's voice came down the line, tension and a hint of panic in his tone. "Can you come to the police station? They've arrested me on suspicion of Nessa's murder."

9

Rupe tried to stay calm as he waited for Jayne to arrive. This was utterly ridiculous. How could they think he was capable of murder? His leg jiggled up and down. *Come on, Jayne.* Where was she? It must have been an hour since he'd called, and she didn't live too far away. Surely, she should have arrived by now.

What if something's wrong? Oh God, what if Kyle had turned up again, and she was having to deal with him instead of coming to Rupe's aid? That would mean he'd have to get another lawyer. He didn't want another lawyer. He trusted Jayne, even more so since their breakthrough date that night.

This wasn't exactly how he'd planned for the evening to end.

Shit. This was serious. Murder. Dear God, he could go to prison. He saw the funny side of most things in life, but there was nothing funny in this. His money might buy him the best legal representation, but it wouldn't help when it came to a jury. And what would his father say? Dad was still grieving after the loss of Mum. The last thing Dad needed was to find out his son was being accused of murder.

Oh, stop rambling, Witters. They're not going to charge you. Jayne would arrive and sort this mess out. It was all just a stupid misunderstanding.

He'd fallen into a false sense of security. When the days had passed without the police asking him any more questions, he'd assumed it was all over—that Nessa had died of natural causes, and the police hadn't thought to tell him.

But if they thought she'd been murdered, then there had to be evidence to suggest such a thing.

A sudden urge to run, to hide—to escape from the situation—built within him like an unstoppable avalanche moving down a mountainside. His heart began to beat faster as adrenaline flooded his bloodstream. This was a nightmare he couldn't wake up from.

He made eye contact with the copper who'd been tasked with babysitting him until Jayne arrived. He tried for a bit of solidarity and understanding. Instead, he got a flat stare and a wide yawn.

The door to the interview room opened, and Jayne walked in. The Jayne of the previous night was gone. In her place stood the super-efficient lawyer, hair swept up and pinned to within an inch of its life, a briefcase clutched tightly in her hand. She wore a smart suit and classy shoes. Relief swept over Rupe.

"A moment with my client, please," she said to the babysitter.

Without a word, the copper stood and left them alone.

"Where the hell have you been?" Rupe bit out, worry and fear making him snap.

Jayne shot him a look from the corner of her eye as she took a pad and pen out of her briefcase. She set the briefcase on the floor and carefully laid out writing materials in front of her before fixing him with a stare.

"You called me forty-five minutes ago. I was in bed. I dressed, gathered my things together, and drove here. That took thirty minutes. Then I had to get through the dick of a desk sergeant downstairs who clearly has a problem with strong, successful women. Anything else?"

Rupe scrubbed his face. "Sorry," he mumbled. "I'm stressing the fuck out."

Jayne squeezed his hand, the comforting gesture of a friend, not a lawyer. "Look, I'll represent you today, but if this does go further, I'm going to pass your case on to my partner."

Rupe shook his head violently. "No. If this does go further—and I hope to fuck it doesn't—I want you."

"But I'm not a criminal lawyer. Darren is a terrific defence attorney."

"No," Rupe repeated firmly. "I want you."

"Let's discuss it later," Jayne said with a tinge of frustration to her tone. "Now remember, stay calm, answer their questions fully, and no smart-arse remarks. Got it?"

"Yeah."

"Then let's get this show on the road."

∼

Detective Fisher entered the room, along with another detective Rupe hadn't seen before. Fisher sat opposite Rupe while the other copper faffed about setting up the tape. Once satisfied, he, too, settled back in his chair.

"I need to inform you that this interview is being recorded. I am Detective Fisher, and this is Detective Armstrong. Can you please identify yourselves for the tape?"

Rupe and Jayne did as he asked.

"Thank you. The time is three oh five a.m."

Fisher reread Rupe his rights.

"Mr Fox-Whittingham, if we can just go over your statement once more, please."

Rupe refrained from rolling his eyes, Jayne's warning loud in his ears. He painstakingly answered their questions, one after the other. After more than an hour of questioning, a knock at the door interrupted Fisher's flow. A female PC put her head inside the interview room and signalled for him to follow her. Fisher stopped the tape and left the room.

Rupe squirmed in his seat as Jayne scratched her pen over the pad in front of her. Her neat swirls and squiggles could end up amounting to the beginning of a defence against a charge for a crime he hadn't committed. People were wrongfully arrested, charged, and convicted all the time.

Nausea churned in his stomach as he waited for Fisher to return. He'd been gone a while, but when the door to the interview room opened and Fisher reentered, something about his demeanour made the hairs on the back of Rupe's neck stand up. Fisher didn't walk back to his chair—he swaggered. After sitting down, he started the tape and repeated who was in the room once again.

"Sorry about that," Fisher said with a false attempt at camaraderie. "We've had the toxicology reports back on Mrs Reynolds." He paused for effect. "She died of a heroin overdose."

Rupe recoiled in his chair. "Heroin? That can't be right. I've never seen Nessa take drugs."

"The toxicology reports confirmed it. A lethal dose. She didn't stand a chance."

"Oh God." A coldness settled over him. Poor Nessa. "But when did she take it? Because I never saw her. She had no needle tracks, no evidence of being a druggie. Something isn't right."

Fisher ignored him. Instead, he passed Rupe a plastic bag that contained a photograph of a guy in his early twenties, maybe younger. The guy looked as rough as they came. He had greasy, lank hair, dirty clothes, an emaciated body, and a wild, almost feral stare as he looked down the camera lens.

"For the tape, I am showing Mr Fox-Whittingham Exhibit 2a. Do you recognise this person?"

"No."

Fisher pushed the photograph closer. "Look again. Make sure, please."

Rupe pressed his lips together, and his face tightened. "I told you, no. I don't recognise him."

"Funny that." Fisher leaned back in his chair. He lifted his chin and smoothed a hand down the front of his pale-blue shirt before tightening his tie. "Because that young man maintains he sold you a half a kilo of heroin the night before Mrs Reynolds died."

Shock rolled through Rupe's system. "I have never seen that person before in my life, and I did *not* buy any heroin from him." He ran a hand over the top of his head. "I wouldn't even know where to buy heroin. Jesus, I'm a businessman, not a druggie in search of a fix, and I don't consort with drug addicts either."

Fisher looked decidedly unimpressed with Rupe's vehement defence. The detective wore a condescending smile. Rupe would have given anything to be able to smack it off his face, but as he was in enough trouble, that wouldn't have been the smartest move.

Rupe turned to Jayne. Her face was unreadable—she'd be a killer poker player—but she had made several notes. Then she focused her gaze on Fisher, her sharp eyes reading his expression.

Fisher waited for a few moments as he let the information sink in, and then he cleared his throat and rose from his chair. "Mr Fox-Whittingham, please follow me to the custody suite, where you will be charged with the murder of Mrs Vanessa Reynolds."

10

Rupe sat in the police cell with his head in his hands, overwhelmed by incredulity. Murder? He couldn't murder someone. Sooner or later, the police would realise their mistake and let him go.

His arse was numb from sitting on the thin mattress. He stood and paced around the cell, not that proper pacing was possible, given the size of the cage. In the corner, a white toilet with a steel rim emitted a faint stench of faeces mingled with bleach. On top of the mattress was a flat pillow covered in stains and a thin, scratchy blanket that would no doubt make him break out in hives.

He couldn't stay there.

As his breathing began to escalate, he forced himself to calm down. Panicking would get him nowhere. He needed to think, to stay focused, to do whatever it took to get out of there as soon as humanly possible.

The letterbox-sized slit in the heavy metal door opened, and the custody sergeant peeked through before the steel bolts holding the door in place slid back. A jolt of hope shot through

Rupe. Maybe they were letting him out after realising they'd fingered the wrong guy.

Instead, the sergeant stepped through the door, holding a plastic tray aloft. "Breakfast," he said, placing the tray on the floor.

Rupe almost laughed. It was like primary school. The food had been placed in individual compartments with overcooked scrambled eggs in one, a slice of bacon in another, and black pudding—disgusting at the best of times—in another. They'd even added a small piece of pineapple coated in congealed yoghurt.

"And a drink." He pointed to a Ribena carton with a red straw sticking out of the top.

The sergeant began to back out of the room, and Rupe had a sudden urge to beg him to stay, but he kept his lips sealed as the heavy steel door was slammed shut.

He stared at the food tray before kicking it aside. He did drink the Ribena, though. And then he sat on the bed and waited.

A couple of hours later, the door to his cell opened once more. The custody sergeant entered, holding a pair of handcuffs.

"Time for court," he said, indicating for Rupe to hold his wrists out. Rupe did as he was asked, his incredulity rising with each step of this godforsaken process. Things like this didn't happen to people like him.

"Where's my lawyer?"

"She'll meet you at court." With his hand on the small of Rupe's back, he ushered him through the door. Outside the police station, Rupe was placed in a prison van—the type with tiny windows that made it impossible to see through, although he, like most people, had seen news footage of photographers desperately scrambling to get a partial shot of the latest newsworthy criminal.

Crap. He'd be newsworthy. The owner of one of the biggest privately owned gaming companies in the world, best buds with a former world number-one tennis player, a father who was an ex-copper. As soon as the press got wind of this, he was fucked.

He wasn't alone in the van. Sitting opposite was a guy in his early twenties who had every inch of his visible skin tattooed, including his face. As he made eye contact with Rupe, he sneered and then made a noise in his throat before landing a large globule of spit on Rupe's shoe. He caught sight of Rupe's face, and he threw back his head and laughed.

Dear God, Jayne. Do your life's best work, and get me the fuck out of here.

A short while later, the van stopped, and the back doors opened. Rupe was led into the courthouse and taken to the cells below ground. After five minutes, Jayne turned up and gave him a reassuring smile as she was let into the cell.

"How are you doing?"

"Terrible. I will get bail, won't I?"

Jayne grimaced. "I'm not sure. I've spoken to Darren, and we've gone through the details of the application, but given the seriousness of the offence, there's no guarantee. It depends on the magistrate we get allocated."

Rupe clutched her arm. "Jayne, you *have* to get me bail. I can't stay in here."

His breathing escalated so quickly that his head began to spin, and he put out an arm to steady himself.

"Hey, stay calm for me, okay?" Jayne's soothing voice broke through his panic. "You're not exactly a flight risk. I'm going to do my best. Are you sure you don't want Darren to represent you?"

Rupe violently shook his head. His hopes plummeted. He was going to prison.

It was another three hours before he was taken from the cells and placed into the square box in the courtroom, an officer close by in case he decided to make a run for it. Rupe focused on the back of Jayne's head as the magistrate called the court to order and the charges were read out.

He could barely take in the words. His head was full of cotton wool as he desperately tried to follow what was going on. Nessa's husband was sitting in the public gallery. Rupe had never seen such loathing on a man's face. He could hardly blame him. Even though their marriage had been for show, according to Nessa, the man must have had some feelings for her. Remorse swept over Rupe. He'd never considered the husband during his trysts with Ness. To him, like his whole fucking life, it had been a bit of a laugh, some fun to liven up his occasional visits to London. What a dickhead he was.

"Rupert Fox-Whittingham. You have been charged with the murder of Mrs Vanessa Reynolds. What is your plea?"

"Not guilty," Rupe replied in a voice that was not his own.

Jayne stood. "Your Honour, I'd like to make an application for bail."

The prosecution lawyer leaped to his feet. "Your Honour, I vehemently oppose. Let's not forget, this is a murder charge."

The magistrate peered over the top of her glasses at the prosecution lawyer. "Thank you for telling me how to do my job, Mr Turner."

As Turner blushed, the magistrate pointed to Jayne. "Well, Ms Seymour. Let's hear it."

Rupe's head began to swim, and Jayne's voice drifted away as she pleaded his case for bail. Christ, prison was a real possibility. Prison. Him. He'd always stayed on the right side of the law. Some of his business dealings pushed the boundaries, but that was what business was about. That was what separated the winners from the losers.

He forced himself to focus on Jayne's appeal on his behalf.

"Your Honour, I will end my application with this. My client is a successful businessman with a clean record. He has various business concerns in the UK, which I submit to the court makes him an unlikely flight risk. In addition, we volunteer to surrender his passport until such time as the trial concludes."

Rupe held his breath, silently willing the magistrate to see things his way. She leaned back in her chair and removed her glasses. After a quick sweep of her hand across her eyes, she replaced them and fixed her gaze on Jayne.

"Given the circumstances and Mr Fox-Whittingham's clean record, bail is granted. Your client will sign in at his local police station every day at four p.m., Ms Seymour. Is that clear?"

"Your Honour, I object," Turner said.

"Duly noted, Mr Turner. Bail stands."

As Rupe's shoulders sagged with relief, he vaguely heard Jayne reply, "Thank you, Your Honour."

He was free.

And now he had to find out what had really happened to Nessa, because as far as the police were concerned, they'd found their culprit.

11

Jayne pushed a large whiskey over the table and sat opposite Rupe, nursing a glass of iced water flavoured with a slice of lemon.

"I owe you, big time," Rupe said, taking a large swig of the amber liquid. As it burned down his throat, he'd never felt more alive.

"Don't get too happy just yet. The hard work is ahead of us. You didn't kill Vanessa Reynolds, but someone did—unless she shot herself full of heroin, which is highly unlikely given what you've told me."

Rupe nodded. "There's no way. Nessa wasn't that sort of girl. She liked a drink, sure, but hard drugs? Not a chance."

"What about the husband?" Jayne said. "That was him in court, correct?"

Guilt swarmed through him once more. "Yeah. I'm not exactly his favourite person."

Jayne's mouth tightened around the edges. "Did he know you were having an affair with his wife?"

"I have no idea. According to Nessa, theirs was a marriage of convenience, although I don't know why they had that sort of agreement. From what she told me, he liked to have a pretty woman on his arm, and in return, she enjoyed the financial security he provided. She did love him, I think, but Nessa was... ahem... a woman with needs, so to speak, and her husband didn't meet them. At least, that's what she told me."

Jayne raised an eyebrow. "He goes down as a person of interest. If he'd been the one in bed with her, he'd have been number one on the police's suspect list."

"Instead, I was the lucky bastard." Rupe shuddered. "I still can't believe I slept next to a dead body."

Jayne flashed him a look of admonishment. "You're all heart, Rupert."

Rupe waved his hand in the air. "Oh, you know what I mean. I'm sorry Nessa is dead. Of course I am, but she wasn't exactly the love of my life, so if you're expecting me to throw myself on her funeral pyre... well, that's unlikely to happen."

She took a sip of water. "Okay, who else? The guy who says he sold you heroin. Are you sure you don't know him?"

"One hundred per cent sure. Not exactly the type of person I mix with."

"Well, we need to find out everything about him and what he's got against you or who paid him to lie."

"Cash has a great PI he's used before. I'll get the guy's number from him."

Jayne tilted her head to the side. "What did your friend need with the services of a private investigator?"

"Oh, Tally—that's his wife—well, they split up in the early stage of their relationship, and she did a runner. Cash hired a PI to track her down."

Jayne's brow furrowed. "A little stalkerish."

Rupe shrugged. "Not really. If you knew them, you'd understand. She's the centre of his whole universe. He lives for her. Their breakup was a complete misunderstanding. There was no way Cash was going to lose the love of his life over a stupid mix-up."

"You're fond of them?"

He nodded. "I haven't even told him what's happened yet. Christ, I haven't even told my dad."

Jayne tapped her pen against her teeth, a habit Rupe had begun to notice and which he found terribly endearing. A frown drifted across her face.

"Have you ever met Detective Fisher before?" she asked.

"No. I've never even had a speeding ticket. Why do you ask?"

"I'm not sure. Something's niggling me. He was completely professional but…" She blew a heavy breath through her nose. "He doesn't like you."

Rupe laughed. "Oh, I got that message, loud and clear. If you ask me, he's one of those guys who despise wealthy people. Works his arse off for sixteen hours a day and barely makes ends meet, so he's bitter about those who have more."

"Maybe." She wrinkled her nose. "There's just something off with that guy. It'll come to me. Probably at three in the morning." She glanced at her watch. "Sorry, I've got to go. I'm back in court this afternoon." She began to gather her papers together. After slotting them in her briefcase, she drank the last of her water and patted his hand. Sparks shot up his arm, and he placed his hand over hers. He fixed his gaze on her.

"Jayne," he began, but he didn't get any further. She pulled her hand out from underneath his and shook her head.

"Don't, Rupe. You're my client, and you're in a lot of trouble. Let's not complicate this."

He swallowed his disappointment. With the arrival of the murder charge, the slim chance of anything happening between them had disappeared. Even if they both wanted to make something happen, he could be looking at fifteen to life. Who would want to stick around for that?

"What happens now?" he said.

"You get the PI that your friend knows onto finding out what he can about the heroin dealer. Might be worth mentioning Fisher to him too. It wouldn't do any harm to know a bit more about him. Make a list of everyone, and I mean everyone, Rupert, who may have a beef with you. Business rivals, ex-girlfriends, jealous husbands."

She raised an eyebrow as Rupe winced at her inference.

"I mean it. I'll go over everything with Darren. I'm also going to talk to a friend I have in the force and see what he can find out about the victim's husband. I'll be in touch."

She rose from her chair. Her hand briefly clasped his shoulder before the gentle touch was gone, and when he turned around, so had she.

Rupe glanced at his watch. Three fifteen. *Better get going.* He had to report in at the cop shop at four, and then he was driving over to Gloucestershire to see Cash and Tally.

~

WHEN RUPE PULLED up outside Cash's home, a sense of calm settled over him. He might not see as much of his friends these days, given how busy they were with the kids, their charity work, and Tally's rather successful writing career, but it didn't matter. Whenever the three of them got together, it was as if they'd never been apart.

Before he'd even reached the front door, Tally had opened it. His godson, Cian, was clinging to her hand, but when he saw Rupe, a broad smile spread across his face. He tore away from Tally's grasp and ran outside.

"Uncle Rupe," he said, flinging himself into Rupe's outstretched arms.

"Hey, buddy. Wow, how big are you getting?" Rupe swung Cian in the air before settling him on top of his shoulders.

"Glad you made it," Tally said, a growing look of concern on her face. "Is everything okay?"

Rupe shook his head slightly to let her know they would need to speak when little ears weren't around.

"Right, come on in," she said. "Cash has taken Darcey to dance lessons, but they should be back in fifteen minutes."

Rupe chuckled at the idea of Cash having to put up with countless excitable little girls all dancing around a studio, no doubt squealing at the tops of their voices. He settled on the couch as Cian begged him to play computer games. He succumbed, and after a few minutes, his shoulders settled into their normal place, and the tension he'd been carrying around since Nessa's death left him.

When Cash got home with Darcey, Rupe played the fun uncle with the two kids until Tally called for bedtime. She hustled the children upstairs while Cash sorted the drinks. Once Tally returned, she and Cash hit Rupe with their perfectly bookended hard stares.

"I've been charged with Nessa's murder."

Tally gasped as her hand flew over her mouth, and Cash straightened up quickly. Rupe could have sworn his spine had been replaced with a steel pole.

"What the fuck?" he bit out.

"Took the words out of my mouth," Rupe said.

Cash frowned. "What evidence do they think they have?"

"She died of a heroin overdose. Apparently, there's a guy who reckons he sold me a truckload of the stuff the day before she died."

"What a crock of shit."

"We know that," Rupe said. "Sadly, the courts are going to need a bit more to go on."

Cash teased his beard with his fingertips. "How's the lawyer working out? If she's no good, I'll give Darren a call and tell him to take over."

A slow grin spread across Rupe's face, despite the fucked-up situation. "Oh no you won't. She's the only good thing to come out of this."

Cash raised an eyebrow. "Even with your life on the line, you're still thinking with your cock."

Rupe laughed. "Like you were any different before you met this gorgeous girl," he said, pulling Tally into a warm hug. As she settled into his side, he could feel her trembling. He kissed her temple. "Don't worry, darling. You know me. I was born lucky." He turned to Cash. "I need the contact details for that PI you've used in the past. Jayne wants him looking into the drug addict to see if he can dig anything up."

Cash nodded. "Frank. He's good. Very thorough and discreet. I'll call him now, set up a meeting at your place for tomorrow."

"At least I got bail. Could have easily been on remand if Jayne hadn't been so bloody brilliant in court."

Tally lifted her head. "Want to stay the night?"

Rupe gave her a squeeze. "Thought you'd never ask."

Tally fetched beers for him and Cash and then left the two of them alone.

"You're so lucky with that one," Rupe said with a fond smile at Tally's retreating back. "I envy you. Marriage, kids, the two of you so happy and settled."

Cash raised an eyebrow. "Don't tell me you're finally growing up, Witters?"

Rupe grinned even as Cash's teasing hit a nerve. "Maybe."

"It'll all work out," Cash said, taking a long pull on his bottle.

"I sure hope so," Rupe said, sounding less than convinced even as he tried to be optimistic.

"Seems to me the police don't have much to go on. A scum-of-the-earth drug pusher fingers a rich, successful businessman? Sounds circumstantial at best. At worst, it's a police fuck-up of epic proportions."

"I was the last to see her alive, and there's no disputing the toxicology reports. I didn't shoot her full of heroin, but unless she did it herself, which I don't believe, someone did."

Cash ran a hand over his face. "You'll tell me if there's anything you need?"

Rupe nodded. "You've already done me a massive favour."

"Oh yeah?"

"I met Jayne."

"You're serious?" Incredulity leaked into Cash's tone.

"Deadly." Rupe swung his bottle in the air before taking a drink. "I feel differently about this one. Unfortunately for me, not only does Jayne vehemently disagree about mixing business with pleasure, but she's also in the middle of a messy divorce from a man who cheated on her, which—given the situation with Nessa—doesn't exactly make me come across as the best choice. Still, I'm working on it."

"Wow," Cash said, a broad grin spreading across his face. "You've joined the *pussy-whipped* club. I've waited years for this."

Rupe flipped his middle finger in the air. "Fuck you," he said to Cash's roaring laughter.

∼

THE FOLLOWING MORNING, Rupe snuck out of the house before the kids woke. He left Tally a thank-you note and a promise to keep Cash up to date. He had to get ready for his meeting with Frank, and he had an urge to see Jayne—an urge that grew with every passing hour. Despite her aversion to having a personal relationship with her client, he couldn't get her out of his head. This was his first experience of a woman burrowing her way beneath his skin, and the feeling was intoxicating and addictive.

The roads were fairly clear until he hit the M4 by Heathrow, and then it took him a good two hours to crawl the last few miles home. Christ, he missed the boat. There were no traffic jams out on the ocean. Given the black cloud hanging over his head, it would be some time before he could experience the freedom of the seas again. As that thought crept into his mind, an overwhelming sense of loss crashed over him. This could be the end of life as he knew it. Regardless of the outcome of the trial, his name would be dragged through the mud, and some of it was bound to stick.

As he entered his house, the smell of strong coffee wafted down the hallway. God bless Abi. The kitchen was empty, but the coffee pot was full. He poured himself a cup and was scrabbling about in the fridge when Abi joined him.

"You're back," she said, giving him a motherly hug even though she was only about ten years older than he. "How are Cash and Tally?"

Rupe extricated himself, but Abi's warm welcome brought a smile to his lips. He was lucky to have her in his corner.

"They're good. Kids too. Listen, Abi, I'm expecting a visitor shortly. When he arrives, can you show him through to the drawing room and then make yourself scarce? Take the rest of the day off."

Abi frowned. "Okay, if you're sure. There's a veggie lasagne in the fridge for your dinner this evening. Just put it in the oven on one eighty for thirty minutes."

"Actually, I'm going out for dinner tonight."

"Oh." She shrugged. "No bother. It'll freeze."

She made Rupe some breakfast, and he took it through into the drawing room. He'd just finished eating when Abi tapped on the door.

"Your visitor is here," she said, waving a medium height, middle-aged guy with grey hair and pronounced jowls into the room.

Rupe stood as Abi closed the door. "Frank," he said, sticking his hand out. "Thanks for coming at such short notice."

"Not at all," Frank replied. "So, Mr Fox-Whittingham. What can I help you with?"

12

Jayne sat in the corner of a coffee shop, waiting for Detective Chief Superintendent Mike Wilson. She twiddled with her necklace and glanced at her watch. Mike was late. It wasn't unusual, but that day his tardiness irritated her. And she knew exactly why.

Jayne didn't get involved with clients. She kept a professional distance, courteous but businesslike. The minute she asked Mike for a favour in relation to Rupe's case, he'd see right through her, and then the questions would start—questions that Jayne didn't have an answer to.

Rupert Fox-Whittingham had done the impossible: he'd snuck beneath Jayne's carefully constructed outer shell. And the worst thing was that he hadn't even had to try very hard. So much for her swearing off men—except she and Rupe were a nonstarter. Relationships between clients and their lawyers weren't forbidden, but they weren't seen as entirely ethical either.

Despite all that, there was something about him, something special and unique that called to a part of Jayne she had buried deep inside. But she couldn't allow him to plough those depths. Rupe was a danger to every promise she'd made to herself.

She'd given her heart and soul away to someone who should have cherished her. Instead, Kyle had taken that gift and destroyed it.

And in the process, her self-esteem and self-worth had taken a hell of a battering.

"Jayne, hi." Mike waved from the doorway of the coffee shop and indicated he was going to get a drink. A few minutes later, he made his way over to her, balancing a latte on a saucer while trying to negotiate the tightly packed-in tables.

"Sorry I'm late," he said as he placed the drink on the table and managed to spill a good portion of the contents. "Dammit." He looked around and spotted the condiment station. He returned with a wad of napkins and mopped up the spillage.

"Sorry," he said again. "Awful morning. Jenna was sick all over me, so I had to get changed. Babies." He rolled his eyes.

Jayne laughed. "How old is she now? Eight, nine months?"

"Eleven months. Can't believe it's gone so quickly."

"Wow, eleven. Time flies."

Mike nodded. "It's been a hell of a ride. You should try it." And then he clapped a hand over his mouth. "Shit. Sorry, Jayne. I'm such a dick. My mind is all over the place."

"It's fine. Old news now."

"Hardly. Nine months is no time at all. How's the divorce going, if you don't mind me asking?"

Jayne grimaced. "It's proving a little tricky."

"Kyle being a knob?"

Jayne laughed. "You could say that."

"Never liked him much," Mike said. "Shifty eyes."

Jayne laughed again, despite being surprised. In all the time she'd known Mike, he'd never once mentioned disliking her husband. "You've been a copper too long, Mike."

"Ain't that the truth." He swept a hand over his tired face. "Only a mere ten years to go until I can draw my pension."

"Counting down already? That's not good."

"Don't get me wrong—I love my job, but now we've got Jenna." He shrugged. "Kind of reorganises your priorities."

"I'm sure it does," Jayne murmured as a wave of regret washed over her. Although she'd never thought about kids—too busy building a career—the fact that she might never have them caused an agonising surge to swell within her. She'd once read some psychobabble about not wanting something until the choice was taken away from you—and then the thing you thought you didn't want became the one most prevalent in your mind.

Mike must have noticed her sad face because he closed a hand over hers. "You'll meet someone else, Jayne. Kyle wasn't the one for you, but the right man is out there somewhere."

Jayne slowly removed her hand from beneath Mike's—although not so fast as to cause offence. His wry smile didn't escape her notice.

"I didn't mean me. Ten years is a long time, Jayne. And in case you hadn't noticed, I'm happily married now."

A flush swept up Jayne's neck and crept over her cheeks. "I know. I'm sorry, Mike. I don't know what's wrong with me."

He leaned back in his chair, the movement clearly meant to give her space. "So what can I do for you?"

Jayne removed a file from her bag. She didn't need the reminder. The contents were firmly fixed in her mind, but referring to the file would show a modicum of professionalism, which might be her saving grace and a way to avoid a grilling.

She opened the file. "I've got a client who's up on a murder charge. Woman in her twenties died of a heroin overdose. My client was the last to see her alive, so naturally, he's the number-one suspect."

"What are you doing covering a criminal case?"

Jayne grimaced. "It's a long story. I did Darren a favour, and now the client doesn't want to switch lawyers. I am capable of providing good counsel."

"I know you are. You're more than capable of turning your hand to anything you choose."

"Thanks," she said with a small smile. "Although I'd appreciate your support on this one. The police reckon they've got a witness who swears he sold my client a half kilo of heroin the night before the woman died."

Mike tapped his fingers against his mouth. "Sounds flaky to me." He held his hand out for the file. Jayne pushed it across the table to him, and Mike began to read—his finger tracing each sentence as he carefully absorbed each word. When he'd finished, he handed the file back to her. "I'm not surprised the judge gave him bail. It's all very circumstantial. I'm intrigued as to why the CPS agreed to take it to court."

"That's what I thought, except the detective in charge seems determined to push it."

"Who's the senior investigative officer?"

"I don't know yet. I've been dealing with a Detective Fisher. He's the one who performed the initial questioning and subsequently charged my client."

"Fisher." Mike scratched his cheek. "He's not one of mine."

"No. The case is being dealt with by Kennington nick. The death occurred on their patch. But I'm hoping you can help me out regardless. I'm after whatever information you can find on the husband."

Mike nodded. "They aren't showing an interest in him?"

"So far, no. They've questioned him, but he has an alibi—whereas my client was in bed with the deceased when she passed. I'm convinced he didn't do it, and I will not let an innocent man be dragged through the courts because some overzealous detective wants to peddle a grudge against rich people."

Mike narrowed his eyes. "Something you want to tell me, Jayne?"

Jayne kept her expression nonchalant. "What do you mean?"

Mike's fingers drummed on the table, his gaze firmly fixed on hers. "How long have we known each other?"

She frowned. "Twelve years."

"Correct. And in all that time, I've never known you get so passionate, so defensive, over a case."

"He's innocent."

"He may well be." Mike's gaze skimmed over her face. "Don't get involved, Jayne."

Jayne picked up the file and slotted it into her bag. She got to her feet. "Thanks for coming, Mike. I know how busy you are."

"Jayne." He wrapped a hand around her wrist as she drew level with him. "Be careful."

Jayne stiffened her spine. "Anything you can find out to help me on this case will be gratefully received, Mike. Poking your nose into my personal life will not be."

She tugged her wrist from his grip and swept past him into the street. As luck would have it, a cab was passing, and Jayne flagged it down. As it drove away, she spotted Mike standing outside the coffee shop, wearing a puzzled look. She groaned. She knew Mike too well. That wouldn't be the end of his prying, despite her sharp reprimand.

13

Rupe picked at his meal, hating every minute of it. Two days had passed since he'd been charged, and during that time, he'd barely seen a soul. He'd never minded the idea of a solitary existence, although in reality, he'd always been surrounded by people. This alien feeling had more to do with his inability to do as he liked because of the damned sign-in at the police station every fricking day.

A sudden urge to see Jayne swept through him. He hadn't heard from her since Monday, and while he could lie to himself and say the real reason for needing to see her was to find out if she'd heard any more on his case, the truth was that without her, he felt as if he'd had a limb amputated. She could push him away all she wanted and toss out lame excuses as to why they couldn't have a relationship, but until she said those things with conviction, he still had a shot at persuading her to give him a chance.

He threw the remains of his dinner in the waste bin and grabbed his wallet and keys. He made a couple of stops on the way over to Jayne's apartment and, an hour later, found himself standing outside, holding a bottle of wine and a large bouquet of flowers. The last time he'd tried to give Jayne flowers, it hadn't worked out so well. Still, second time lucky and all that.

He knocked on the door and waited. A few seconds later, Jayne opened it and let out an exasperated sigh. "Can't you take a hint?"

He thrust the flowers at her and sauntered inside. "I'm fine with hints. It's blatant warnings that I find a challenge. Something about being told no just makes me want to work harder at persuading you to say yes."

He removed a couple of wine glasses from the kitchen cupboard and poured full measures of the crisp Chablis, one of his favourites from Fortnum's. When he turned around, Jayne was still standing by the door, a vexed look on her face.

"You can't simply come around here unannounced whenever you feel like it."

"I did announce," he said, walking back into the living area of her apartment. "I texted you, and I knocked just then."

Jayne strode towards a nearby table and snatched up her phone. She frowned at the screen before turning her trademark glare on him. "You are the most exasperating man I've ever met."

Rupe clutched his chest. "That's the nicest thing you've ever said to me. I think I'm in love."

Jayne made a noise that sounded remarkably like a growl. Rupe grinned. "Here, darling, have a glass of wine. Take the edge off your temper."

She snatched the glass from his hand and dumped the flowers in the sink. Then she turned around and pressed her ramrod-straight back against the wall on the far side of the kitchen as though to put distance between them and anchor herself at the same time.

"What do you want, Rupert?"

He tilted his head to one side. "You."

She sighed, but her face did soften slightly. "We've had this conversation."

"No," Rupe replied. "We haven't. You told me it's a no-no, and I've decided to ignore you." He set his wine down on a side table and casually walked towards her. After removing the glass from her clenched fist, he reached into her hair.

"What are you doing?" she said although she didn't stop him.

Rupe ignored her and began to remove the bobby pins holding her updo in place. When he'd removed every one, he ruffled her hair and draped the golden locks over her shoulders. "Better. Makes you much less austere."

"I prefer professional," she bit back, making him chuckle.

He picked up her wine glass and took her hand in his before leading her over to the couch. The expected resistance didn't come, and as Rupe sat down, tugging Jayne beside him, he pressed the glass back into her hand and reached around for his own.

"I know you've been hurt, Jayne, but not all men are like Kyle. Please don't shut yourself off from possibilities simply because you chose the wrong one first time around."

She drew her teeth across her bottom lip, causing his eyes to drift to her mouth. "This is about the fact that you're my client, not my crumbling marriage."

"You can lie to yourself all you want, but there is nothing to stop us having a relationship if that's what we want to do. You're using the client-lawyer argument as a way of avoiding the fact that you're attracted to me. Don't deny it," he said, holding his hand up as she began to speak. "I know, Jayne. I see it. I *feel* it."

She froze as he gently stroked her cheek with the back of his hand.

"Take a risk. Might turn out to be the best thing you've ever done."

He leaned in—slowly, because he got the feeling that if he moved too quickly, she'd scarper like a deer hearing a twig snap in the woods. He gently cupped her chin and, with the softest of touches, brushed his lips over hers. His stomach clenched as electricity sparked between them. When she didn't pull away, he edged closer. His hand curved around the back of her neck, and he drew her mouth to his, deepening the kiss. Blood rushed to his groin so fast his head began to spin. Dear God, he'd never experienced a reaction like *that* to a first kiss.

A low groan eased from his throat. He kept one hand firmly around her neck. His other moved to her waist. Encouraged by her acceptance of his mouth on hers, he ran the tip of his tongue over her bottom lip.

She tore away and scrambled to her feet. With her arms wrapped around her body, she hugged herself. "I'd like you to leave please."

Rupe frowned. "What did I do?"

"I told you. I don't want this, and I don't want you. Now, please leave. I have work to do. On *your* case," she added forcefully.

"Jayne." Rupe reached for her as he got to his feet.

Her hand shot up, palm facing him. "I said go."

Rupe shook his head. He turned to leave but then paused and faced her once more. She hadn't moved from the same spot, her arms still protectively around her body.

"You might be doing your best to ignore what's happening between us, but at some point, you're going to have to face your feelings. All it takes is a touch of bravery. Dig deep, Jayne, because I'm going nowhere."

∽

JAYNE ALMOST REOPENED her apartment door after Rupe had left just so she could slam it. His reasonableness at her rejection of his advances was frustrating as hell. She'd expected him to argue, to try to persuade her, to do something. Instead, he'd simply backed away and done as she asked.

The problem was she didn't want him to back away. Not really. But fear of her growing feelings for a virtual stranger had made her backpedal at an alarming rate. She *couldn't* get involved with a client. Her career and her morals were all she had left, not to mention that Rupert Fox-Whittingham had absolutely no integrity. He'd been sleeping with a married woman, for goodness' sake. Men like him hurt women like her.

She touched her fingertips to her lips. Even though she'd sensed him holding back, that brief kiss had given her a glimpse into what he was capable of. Her core tightened as she relived the moment, but at the back of her mind, an insistent voice kept telling her to reject him.

Even if she could get past the complication of Rupe being a client, it was far too soon to think about starting a new relationship—wasn't it? Nine months wasn't long at all, although when she had more honest conversations with herself, she could admit that her marriage to Kyle had broken down long before his affair with Flick. The signs of her reluctance to be around him had been there—her preference to stay at work rather than go home, or the way she took on extra cases, which meant having to work weekends. And even when she finished early, she would take the long way back to their apartment, occasionally getting off the tube three or four stops early and walking the rest of the way.

Jayne covered her face with her hands and rubbed hard. It had been so long since anyone had shown her any tenderness that she'd forgotten how addictive it could be. Already, she was craving more of it, and that was a dangerous road to begin travelling down.

Despite the early hour, Jayne headed off to bed. She took Rupe's case files with her as though they somehow brought him closer. She reread all of the statements, including going over Rupe's three times. There had to be something that she was missing.

Frustrated, she stuffed the papers back into the folder and dropped it on the floor. She burrowed under the covers and closed her eyes, but then her phone rang. She cursed as she slipped a hand from beneath the quilt and felt around for it.

"What?" she snapped without even looking at the caller ID.

"I'm just calling to say goodnight."

Rupe's gentle voice soothed her, and she curled onto her side and pressed the phone harder to the side of her head, creating a greater connection between them. A tear slipped from the corner of her eye, dampening her pillow. Something in his voice made her want to bawl her eyes out, to beg him to come over. But she couldn't do it.

"I'll see you tomorrow, Jayne."

Even though they had no professional reason to do such a thing, Jayne found herself saying, "Yes, Rupe. I'll see you tomorrow."

14

Rupe entered the coffee shop, immediately spotting Kyle sitting at a small, round table squished in the corner. The man flashed an irritated look at his watch. Rupe inwardly grinned. He'd purposely kept Kyle waiting. For all Rupe gave a shit, the fucker could wait all day.

Rupe sidled through the tables and pulled out the chair opposite Kyle, the scraping noise causing him to raise his head.

"You're late," Kyle snapped.

Rupe eased into the chair, legs splayed wide. "That looks painful." He gave a false smile and tilted his head at Kyle's busted nose and black eyes.

Kyle glowered. "It is, which is why you're going to pay."

Rupe kept his body loose. "Now, now. That's no way to begin a negotiation."

"Your choice. I can always still go to the police."

Rupe stood. "You do that." He turned to leave.

"Wait," Kyle said.

Rupe glanced over his shoulder.

"You have to admit I'm owed something for this." Kyle pointed at his face.

Rupe placed the tips of his fingers on the table and loomed over Kyle. "When you put your hands on a woman in anger, you're not owed a goddamn thing. You got exactly what you deserved. In fact, you got off lightly."

Kyle expelled a breath through his nose. "I shouldn't have done that to Jayne," he said through gritted teeth.

Sensing an easy win, Rupe sat back down. "No. You shouldn't have."

"I still think I should get something. You did assault me after all."

Rupe took a pen out of the inside pocket of his suit jacket and reached for a napkin. "I'm already bored with your company, so here's how this is going to go down. I will write a number on here." He shook the napkin in the air. "It will be my one and only offer. You are going to accept it. And then you are going to take a *reasonable* divorce settlement. I'd prefer it if you didn't get one penny, but that would look odd to Jayne."

"And if I don't?" Kyle said.

Rupe slowly grinned. He leaned forward and rested his forearms on the table. "Let me paint you a scenario. You're a bug, scuttling around on the floor. Hovering over you is a great big fucking boot. That boot can choose to come down hard and end you, or it can let you scurry away with the morsel of food. Your choice."

Rupe scrawled a number on the napkin and set it in front of Kyle. He stared at it. As the seconds scraped by, Rupe began drumming his fingers on the table. "My time is valuable, unlike yours. In ten seconds, I'm leaving, and that offer will no longer be valid."

When Kyle remained silent, Rupe pushed back his chair.

"Fine," Kyle spat out. "Deal."

"See, Kyle, you're not so dumb after all." Rupe got to his feet. "There's one more thing. You are to stay away from Jayne. If I hear you've been anywhere near her, now or in the future, I will make you sorrier than you can imagine." He picked up his pen and slotted it into his inside pocket. "My lawyer will be in touch. Nice doing business with you."

He left the coffee shop with a broad grin on his face and climbed into his waiting car. Winning was so much fun.

15

"So have you found anything out?" Jayne said to Frank, Rupe's PI.

The three of them had met up in a local pub not far from Jayne's apartment. The place smelled of stale beer and cigarette smoke. Even though it was illegal to light up inside public places, Rupe guessed it was one of those pubs that had a few lock-ins where the rule of law was ignored.

"I tracked down the pusher. It wasn't that difficult from the information you gave me. He maintains he sold you the heroin," Frank said to Rupe. "But when I showed him four photos and asked him to pick you out, he couldn't."

"Surely the police would have done the same thing?" Rupe said, looking over at Jayne with a perplexed expression.

"You'd think," Frank said.

Jayne made a note in her journal. "The list of questions I have for Detective Fisher is growing by the minute. The more I look into this, the shakier the ground this case seems to be built upon."

"Ah yes, Detective John Fisher." Frank moved their drinks to the side of the table and set down a folder. "Now, this is much more interesting. I did as you asked and looked into his background." He pulled out a sheet of paper and began to read. "His parents were hard-working people. His mother was a nurse until she retired in 2007. His father was a supervisor at a factory that made cardboard boxes until he was made redundant five years ago when the factory closed down. Since then, he's worked odd jobs here and there but nothing permanent.

"They live in a two-up two-down terraced house in Croydon. They still have a small mortgage on the property, but the mother's pension and the father's modest income mean they can afford the repayments."

Rupe frowned. "Sorry to sound like an arse, but this is pertinent how?"

Frank gave Rupe a condescending look. "When researching someone's background, Mr Fox-Whittingham, it is important to check all the strands of a person's life. Please, if you'll let me continue."

Rupe spotted Jayne's twitching lips and stuck out his tongue. Frank didn't notice the exchange as he pressed on.

"Detective Fisher is their oldest child at thirty-eight. He's been in the force since he was nineteen. When he reached the rank of detective five years ago, his career stalled. It seems our detective friend has a bit of a chip on his shoulder. Tells anyone who'll listen that if his parents were middle class, he'd be at least a DCI by now."

"Ha," Rupe said, flashing a triumphant look at Jayne, who shook her head at him. Frank continued as though Rupe hadn't interrupted. Clearly, the PI was a man on a mission.

"His parents had three other children: David, who is thirty-five and works for the post office, Rory, thirty-two, who is a retail assistant, and the youngest, Julie, who died a year ago when she was twenty-nine."

"Died?" Jayne and Rupe said simultaneously.

"Of what?" Jayne continued.

"Suicide," Frank said.

"How awful," Rupe muttered.

Jayne began to scrawl in her journal, but Frank stopped her. "I'll give you all my notes. No need to make extra."

"Terrible for the parents," Jayne said, putting her pen down. "Suicide is never easy for those left behind. They always seem to blame themselves."

Frank searched through his folder once more and pulled out a photograph of a pretty young girl. She had straight coffee-coloured hair and soft brown eyes and wore a yellow dress that made her tanned skin stand out. She was smiling into the camera and looked happy and relaxed. Frank pushed the photo in front of Rupe.

"This is Julie. Do you recognise her?"

Rupe barely looked at the photograph. "No. Why would I?"

"Because she worked for one of your businesses here in London."

Rupe's eyebrows shot up, nearly disappearing into his hairline. "She worked for me? Wow, small world. I still don't know her. I have over twenty thousand people who work for my different businesses globally. I can't know them all."

"Ah yes, but Julie is a little different. You see, a month before she killed herself, you fired her."

Rupe's head flinched back as his mind began to race. He'd never seen the girl in his life, so how could he have fired her? He gave Frank an astonished look. "I can't have done. I would have remembered something like that. Firing an employee is extremely rare."

He picked up the photograph and gave it a more detailed look. Nope, nothing about the girl triggered any memory at all.

"Which of my companies did she work for?"

"FW Game World Limited," Frank replied.

"Why was she fired?"

Frank shook his head. "I haven't been able to find out. I was rather hoping you'd tell me."

Rupe scratched his cheek. None of this made any sense. He took out his phone and snapped a picture of the girl in the photograph. He rose from his seat. "Give me a minute. I'm going to call the director of that division and see if he can shed some light on what's gone on."

Rupe stepped outside the pub. He stood off to one side, away from the smokers gathered around the entrance. These last few weeks, his life had taken on the feeling of an alternate reality. Dead bodies, arrests, murder charges, police cells, court, and now it seemed that he had an unknown connection to the lead detective on his case. Not to mention Jayne and his increasing attraction towards her. No wonder his head was spinning.

Rupe found the name he was looking for in his contact list and hit the call button. He tapped his foot as he waited.

Eventually Aaron, the head of his London branch, answered. "Hey, Rupe," he said, his voice light, bright, energised. "How's things?"

Fucking awful. "Not bad. How's business?"

"Growing every day, my friend," Aaron said. "Are you in London?"

"Yeah. I'll swing by early next week."

"Before you head back to the yacht—hey, you lucky bugger."

Rupe didn't care to enlighten him about his current turn of bad luck. "Listen, Aaron, does the name Julie Fisher ring a bell?"

"Julie Fisher, Julie Fisher," Aaron muttered under his breath. Rupe could imagine him, eyes raised to the ceiling as he tried to locate the right file in his brain. "Not offhand. Why?"

"I'm sending you a picture. Let me know when you get it."

Rupe forwarded the photograph of Julie to Aaron's number. After a few seconds, Aaron said, "Got it." There was a pause. "Aha. Yes, I remember her now, although she went by the name of Julie Fraser, not Fisher."

"But it's definitely her?"

"Oh, yeah," Aaron said, his voice taking on a harder edge. "I never forget a thief."

"Thief? What do you mean?"

"She was caught trading software code for an upcoming release with one of our rivals. Silly woman. She should have known we'd have had programs that would pick such activity up. Fortunately, we caught her before she did any real damage."

"Why don't I know about this?" Rupe said as irritation began to prickle beneath his skin—irritation at himself. How could he have dropped the ball on something so important?

"You do know," Aaron said. "I might not have given you a blow-by-blow account, but I emailed you about what she'd done, and you agreed with my decision to fire her."

"Can you reforward the email to me?"

Fuck, he'd messed up. He had absolutely no recollection of an important issue in one of his main branches.

"Of course. Rupe?" Aaron's voice took on a note of concern. "Is something wrong?"

"Did you involve the police over the incident?"

"No. She begged me not to. Said her brother was a copper, and she was worried it would affect his promotion chances. Because there hadn't been a financial loss, I agreed. I did tell her that I'd make sure she didn't get a job at another software company, though."

"Fair enough," Rupe said.

"Why are you raising this?"

"She killed herself."

Aaron gasped. "No."

"Yep. One month after you fired her, it seems."

"Shit. That's awful."

"Locate the email, and send it to me straight after this call. It's quite urgent, Aaron."

"Sure thing." His voice had become quieter, more reflective, tinged with guilt. "I made the right decision, though. I couldn't condone theft."

"You did the right thing," Rupe said. *It's me who's been doing the wrong things.* "I'll be in touch."

Rupe headed back into the pub, a heavy weight pressing down on him. Could Fisher be so distraught about his sister's suicide that he'd set up Rupe for murder as payback? And how did Nessa and her husband fit into this? Christ, trying to figure it all out was making his head hurt.

Jayne and Frank were exactly where he'd left them, their body language awkward, like two strangers trying to connect through small talk. As Rupe approached, Jayne turned her head and gave him a grateful look.

"Find out anything?" she said, moving her drink out of his way.

"Yeah." Rupe ran a weary hand over his face as he recounted his conversation with Aaron. "I'm going to go over there on Monday and see if I can talk to some of her colleagues. Aaron is sending across the email where I apparently agreed with his decision to fire her." He made eye contact with Jayne before turning his attention to Frank. "Do you think a copper would go as far as setting up a stranger for murder because he laid the death of his sister at that person's door?"

Frank pulled a face. "I've seen less tenuous reasons for revenge."

"Jesus."

Jayne got to her feet. "I'm going to talk to Mike again. This potentially changes everything. I'll see if he's been able to look into the information Fisher submitted to his superiors and the CPS in order to get this case to court."

Frank also rose from his chair and stuck out his hand. "If you need anything else, Mr Fox-Whittingham, you have my number."

16

Jayne tore up the stairs, taking them two at a time. She strode down the hallway towards Mike's office, a young police officer trailing in her wake.

"Ms Seymour," he called out hopefully. "Hold on please, ma'am."

Jayne ignored him and upped her pace.

Outside Mike's office, his PA scrambled to her feet as she spotted Jayne on a collision course. "Wait, please," she said, sticking out her arm.

"I need to see Detective Chief Superintendent Wilson right away," Jayne said, her tone barely controlled.

"He's in a meeting right now. If you'll take a seat."

"I'm sure he'll want to hear what I have to say." Ignoring the open-mouthed horror of Mike's assistant, Jayne knocked once before pushing open Mike's office door.

Three pairs of eyes swivelled in her direction.

"Sorry to interrupt," she said as the PA hovered to her right, mumbling apologies that weren't hers to make. "I need a word with you." Jayne fixed a stare on Mike. "Urgently."

"Jayne, can you please wait outside," Mike said through

gritted teeth, his face pale, apart from two angry pink splodges on his cheeks. "I'm in a meeting."

"You're going to want to hear what I have to say, Mike."

He half rose from his seat. "I am in a meeting with Assistant Commissioner Grimwald and Deputy Assistant Commissioner Saunders. Wait outside. Now." His tone was adamant. As Jayne made eye contact with the two seniors filling Mike's office, they looked even less impressed with her uninvited interruption than Mike had been.

"Sorry," she said even as she straightened her spine in an unapologetic show. "I'll be right outside," she added firmly for Mike's benefit.

Mike's PA gave her a withering glance before burying her head in her computer, her fingers flying across the keyboard as she noisily typed. The young policeman who'd escorted her to the chief superintendent's office bounced from foot to foot as if wondering what to do next. Eventually, he mumbled something about paperwork and left.

Jayne paced, hating the cooling of heels that had been foisted upon her. After fifteen minutes, the door to Mike's office opened, and the assistant commissioner and deputy assistant commissioner walked out, both looking sombre. They didn't even glance in her direction as they set off down the hall. Mike cocked his head, signalling for her to follow him.

Before he'd even slammed the door behind her, he bellowed, "What the *fuck* was that, Jayne? Thank you very much for embarrassing me in front of not just my boss, but my boss's boss. Jesus!"

Jayne nibbled on her bottom lip. "Sorry, Mike. Really. But something has come up in relation to the case I spoke to you about."

Mike narrowed his eyes. The tinge of red on his cheeks had travelled and now covered his entire neck in angry blotches. "The fact that you have an obvious sidebar going on with your client does *not* give you the right to barge into my office and behave in such an adolescent manner. Nor does our history."

Jayne straightened. "Firstly, there is *nothing* going on between my client and me. And secondly, our history? We don't have a history, Mike. We have a professional relationship where I scratch your back and you scratch mine, when needed. A drunken pass years ago from a man who should have known better does not constitute a history."

Mike lowered himself into his chair, his hands gripping the arms until his knuckles turned white. "Well, Jayne, if you're looking for my help, you're not going about it the right way."

Jayne sat in one of the two chairs opposite, the leather still warm from its previous occupant—an errant observation that was not in the least bit welcome. She squirmed and perched her backside on the very edge.

"I'm sorry," she said again, this time with more feeling.

Mike steepled his fingers under his chin. "I've never seen you like this, Jayne. This guy must be something special to ruffle your feathers on this scale."

An uncomfortable feeling stirred in Jayne's gut. She was unwilling to acknowledge her innermost thoughts to herself, let alone share them with anyone else. "Rubbish," she said, waving her hand dismissively in the air. "Hear me out, please."

Mike nodded, his keen blue eyes focused on Jayne as she relayed what Rupe had found out about Fisher. When she finished, Mike leaned back in his chair and threaded his hands behind his head.

"Well?" Jayne said when Mike remained silent. "It's a conflict of interest at best. And it brings into question the entire case evidence against my client."

"It's not ideal, I'll give you that."

"Not ideal?" Jayne scoffed. "The man has a clear vendetta against my client. I want him immediately suspended. I want someone else reviewing the evidence, and then I want this case dropped."

"Steady on," Mike said. "I can't simply jump to conclusions on your say-so."

Jayne's skin began to prickle as rage boiled up inside her. *Stay calm.*

"Are you questioning my word?" she said, her voice trembling with an undercurrent of warning.

"No. I'm saying I need to look into things before I can act. Leave it with me."

As Jayne began to speak, Mike held up his hand. "I said, leave it with me."

Doing her best to curb her growing anger, Jayne rose from her seat. She leaned forward, placing both hands flat on Mike's desk. "Twenty-four hours, Mike. I'll be back tomorrow. I don't care that it's Saturday. I'm sure you agree this is best dealt with quickly. We don't want the press finding out about a bent police officer."

Mike's face smouldered beneath a chilly expression. His lips were pressed into a flat line, his eyes narrowed to slits as he studied her face in silence. His chest rose and fell as he took a couple of deep breaths, clearly trying to calm himself down. Jayne inwardly cursed. She should have known better—Mike wasn't the type to respond well to threats. She needed him to play ball, and she needed him on her team.

She softened her features. "I'm sorry. That was out of order. You know I'd never leak something like that to the press, and it's not my place to make demands. I know how busy you are, but I'd appreciate it if you could look into this matter as soon as possible. An innocent man's freedom is on the line here, not to mention his reputation."

Mike blew out a soft breath through his nose, and his lips curved into a wry smile. "You always could wrap me around your little finger, Jayne. I'll look into it, but it'll be Monday. I've promised Tanya that I'll take her and Jenna to the beach this weekend. I'll call you as soon as I know anything."

Jayne walked around to Mike's side of the desk and planted a quick kiss on his cheek. "You're a legend," she said with a smile.

Mike rolled his eyes, but he didn't look displeased. "Get out of here, woman. I've got a job to do."

Jayne picked up her handbag. "When this is over, drinks are on me," she said as she left Mike's office.

She darted downstairs, the heavy weight on her shoulders lifting slightly. Mike's job these days might involve pushing papers and managing ever-decreasing budgets, but in his heart, he was still a copper and one of the best. If anyone could get to the bottom of this in record time, it was Mike.

As soon as Jayne cleared the building, certain she was out of earshot, she called Rupe. Time to give him a piece of good news that he could cling to.

17

Rupe woke on Saturday morning feeling much more positive, even though his situation hadn't altered one bit. The chief superintendent Jayne had referred to the previous day was fairly influential by all accounts. If he was getting involved in Rupe's case, that could only be a good thing.

He sprang out of bed. After showering in record time, he gave himself a close shave and added a light touch of cologne. He'd made no particular arrangements to see Jayne, but as he'd ruined last weekend for her, he intended to make up for that by offering to drive her to see her grandmother.

He sent her a text, informing her that he was on his way over. He wasn't sure what kind of a response he'd get, but when she replied with *Bring croissants*, he couldn't stop the broad smile from spreading across his face.

Despite being early, it was already hot. Rupe wandered around the side of the house and pressed the button to open the garage door. As the mechanism whirred, a stir of excitement churned in his gut.

He scanned the lineup of cars in his garage before picking the BMW M4 Convertible. Imagining Jayne's hair blowing in the breeze made him harden in his jeans. The one kiss they'd shared had left him desperate for more, even if she had virtually thrown him out when he'd tried to deepen it. By agreeing he could go over that morning, maybe she had finally decided to stop fighting their obvious attraction to one another.

He stopped by a bakery and picked up a selection of pastries and a couple of coffees. He took the lift up to Jayne's floor and balanced the bag of pastries on top of the coffee cups as he knocked on her door.

His eyes widened when she greeted him. She was dressed in a pair of red shorts and a tight white T-shirt that clung to her breasts. Her long legs were bare, and on her feet were Roman-style sandals. Her hair was pulled back into a high ponytail. The whole effect made her look about twenty. His pulse jolted.

"About time," she said, reaching for the bag of food. "I'm starving." She appeared not to notice his nonplussed state as she wandered into the kitchen and began taking plates out of the cupboard.

Rupe managed to drag himself back to the present. He stepped inside and closed the door behind him. By the time he'd reached the kitchen, Jayne was coming towards him with two plates piled high with warm pastries.

"Here." She thrust a plate at him and swapped it for a coffee. She wandered past and sat down on the sofa, crossing her legs in front of her. As she tucked into a pain au chocolate, she made an appreciative sound at the back of her throat. Rupe's cock twitched, and he suppressed a groan as she delicately wiped crumbs from the side of her mouth with her little finger.

"These are amazing." As she realised he was still standing like an idiot with a plate in one hand and a coffee in the other, she frowned. "What's up with you?"

Rupe coughed and went to sit down. "Nice outfit." He balanced his coffee in his lap and took a bite out of an almond croissant.

Jayne glanced down at herself before looking up with a girlish grin. "It's nice to dress down on the rare occasions I'm not working."

Rupe lazily swept a gaze over her. "If you're going to look like that, you need to not work more often."

A faint tinge of red touched her cheeks before she recovered her composure. She took another bite of her croissant.

"Listen," Rupe said. "I totally ruined last weekend for you what with my being up on a murder charge and all. How do you feel about letting me drive you to your grandmother's today?"

Jayne grimaced at his murder charge comment, and then her eyes widened in surprise. "You'd do that?"

Rupe shrugged one shoulder. "Sure. I'll drop you off, wander around for a bit, and pick you up later. A quick dinner, then we can head home."

Jayne grinned. "What if I told you my grandmother lives in Scotland?"

"Then I'll take you to Scotland, although it might be a bit of a stretch to travel there and back in a day." He waggled his eyebrows. "We'd need an overnight stay."

"Lucky for me she only lives in Kent, then," Jayne said, playfully bumping her shoulder against his.

Rupe gave her a faux-aggrieved look. "You've wounded me, Jayne Seymour."

She rolled her eyes. "Sure I have." And then she frowned. "What about your sign-in at the police station?"

Rupe clapped a hand to his forehead. "Shit. I'd completely forgotten about that. Do you think they'll let me sign in at one local to your grandmother's?"

"Let's call in to the police station first. I doubt they'll have a problem with it."

Jayne brushed pastry crumbs off her T-shirt. She stood and held out her hand for his plate.

"Right then," she said after she'd put the dirty dishes in the dishwasher. "Let's go."

They strolled downstairs in amiable silence, but when Jayne laid eyes on his car, she chuckled under her breath. "You are such a cliché."

Rupe opened her car door and waved his arm with a flourish. "At the risk of damaging your feminine sensibilities, after you."

Jayne slipped inside the car. "Ow," she said as her bare legs touched the hot leather seat. She lifted her backside in the air.

Rupe climbed in beside her and reached between the seats. He passed her a folded-up towel. "Sorry, the leather gets a bit hot. It'll cool down as we get going."

Jayne laid the towel beneath her and sat back down. "Better. I'll send you the bill for my skin grafts."

Rupe leaned towards her. "Don't worry, darling," he whispered in her ear. "I'll rub some salve into them later."

Jayne shoved him away. "Get going before I change my mind."

Rupe laughed and started the car. As they pulled away from the kerb, he spotted Kyle walking along the street. Rupe glanced at Jayne. She'd noticed him too. She quickly ducked down in her seat.

"Put your foot down. He's the last person I want to deal with when I'm in such a good mood."

Rupe obliged, even though Jayne had nothing to fear from Kyle any longer. Rupe had made sure of that. As he pressed the accelerator, the car jumped forward, and they sped away. Jayne pushed herself upright.

"Have you heard anything from him?" she said.

Rupe shook his head.

"You will. It's a bit late for him to go to the police, but he'll definitely pursue you for a financial settlement."

Rupe kept his face straight. He'd tell her at some point in time, just not right then. As he spotted her still waiting for an answer, he gestured dismissively. "It doesn't matter." He chuckled.

"A few years ago, Cash punched a reporter at a press conference for dissing an article which Tally, his wife, had written. She's a journalist," he added for context. "Cash had had trouble with this particular reporter for years. He paid him off, and the problem went away. Cash reckoned it was worth every penny because each time he recalled seeing the guy's nose splattered across his face, it made him smile. I'm starting to understand what he meant."

Jayne laughed, and the carefree sound did funny things to Rupe's insides. He glanced sideways. Her ponytail was swinging in the wind, her cheeks were tinged pink, and she looked more relaxed than she had at any time since he'd known her.

Fortunately, the police agreed he could sign in at a different station, and after the arrangements had been made, they set off for Kent. As they left London behind, the roads narrowed and the traffic lessened. Rupe put on some music, and Jayne leaned back her head and closed her eyes, her lips moving silently as she mouthed the words to the songs. Contentment washed over him. Up until then, he might not have been the settling-down type, but something about being with Jayne was making him question the validity of his previous choices. Sooner or later, he'd have to grow up, and if Jayne was the one who forced that change through, he wouldn't be complaining.

As they got closer to the village of Hawkhurst, where Jayne's grandmother lived, Rupe slowed the car and turned down the music. Jayne had fallen asleep on the journey, so he gently shook her arm to rouse her.

"We're almost there. Can you direct me to your grandmother's house?"

Jayne rubbed her eyes and sat up straight. "Wow, sorry to fall asleep. I'm not a very good road-trip companion, am I?"

Rupe glanced sideways. "You snore terribly. I had to turn the music up."

"I do not snore," Jayne said in an indignant tone, her arms folded across her chest.

"Oh yes you do. If I hadn't known better, I'd have assumed we were driving through a building site. You're like a pneumatic drill when you get going."

Jayne shot him a withering look. "Well, count yourself lucky it's the one and only time you'll have to listen to it."

Rupe flashed a wolfish grin. "I wouldn't be so sure about that."

She shook her head in defeat. "Keep going down this road. At the end, turn left, and I'll direct you from there."

After five minutes, she instructed him to stop outside a whitewashed cottage. The front garden was small but well tended, with potted plants and gravel instead of a lawn. Low maintenance, he guessed, for an old lady to manage.

Jayne climbed out of the car while Rupe stayed where he was. As she began to walk to the front door, she glanced over her shoulder.

"Well, come on, then," she said. "You might as well meet Ganny and have a cup of tea."

Rupe grinned. "Wow. Two glasses of wine the other night, and now I'm meeting the family. Surely, this puts me in the middle of that inner circle of yours."

She raised her eyes heavenward. "Not even on the periphery. I simply thought that offering you a drink was the least I could do, considering you've driven me all the way down here." She shrugged. "Of course, if you'd rather not..."

Rupe scrambled out of the car, and as he drew level with Jayne, he knitted his fingers through hers.

She raised an eyebrow. "Down, boy," she said, extricating herself as the front door opened. Jayne threw herself into the outstretched arms of her grandmother. It was several seconds before they broke apart.

"Ganny, you look wonderful," Jayne said, holding her grandmother at arm's length. She glanced at him. "This is a friend of mine, Rupert Fox-Whittingham. Rupe, this is my grandmother, Sally."

"It's good to meet you, Sally," Rupe said, his hand outstretched. Sally shook it as her keen hazel eyes—a replica of Jayne's—swept over him. Rupe got the sense he was being assessed. Clearly, Jayne had inherited her ability to read people from her grandmother. After a few seconds of silence, Sally muttered under her breath, "Better than the other deadbeat," before turning her back on them. She ambled into the living room.

"You passed the test," Jayne murmured under her breath as they followed her grandmother. "Ganny never did like Kyle."

Rupe lowered his voice. "Wine, meeting the family, and being approved of by said family. I am on *fire*."

Jayne dug her elbow hard in his ribs, and he groaned.

"Have I told you I like it rough?" he whispered in her ear.

"Shhh," she said, hitting him with a look of admonishment as her grandmother wandered into the kitchen to make tea.

After being grilled by Jayne's grandmother for thirty minutes, Rupe made his excuses and left them to it. He needed to check in at the police station, and Jayne deserved some downtime with her only family. She didn't need him cramping her style. He promised to return in a few hours to take her home. On their way back, he planned to take her on a slight detour to a fabulous fish restaurant a few miles farther down the coast.

Jayne was definitely softening towards him, and he was determined to take advantage of that. Sure, he still had the murder charge hanging over his head—which neither of them had mentioned to Jayne's grandmother—but there was no use moping. He couldn't stop his whole life because of something that he had absolutely no control over other than what he and Jayne were already doing to try to prove his innocence.

He arrived to pick up Jayne just before five. Her grandmother saw them off with warnings about driving carefully. Jayne twisted in her seat and waved until her grandmother's house disappeared from view.

Facing forwards again, she let out a contented sigh. "Thank you for bringing me," she said with a smile that made his stomach do a backflip. "She might act tough, but since my grandfather died, she's definitely frailer."

"How long ago did he die?"

"Four years." Sadness swept across her face. "I miss him terribly but not as much as she does. They were married for fifty-five years."

Rupe gently squeezed her fingers but didn't linger. However, when he rested his hand on top of the gear lever in his preferred driving style, Jayne covered it with hers.

"You're a good person, Rupert Fox-Whittingham."

A delightful shiver ran up his spine, and he turned his palm up so he could hold her hand. "Hungry?"

"Starving."

"Good. I've booked us a table at a restaurant on the coast. We should be there in about half an hour."

∼

THE RESTAURANT WAS SITUATED DIRECTLY on the beach, and Rupe had secured them a table on the outside veranda, where they could smell the sea and hear the waves lapping on the shore. After they'd eaten, Rupe suggested a walk along the promenade. To his surprise and delight, Jayne agreed. A light breeze blew off the water, and when Jayne shivered, Rupe took a risk by putting his arm around her waist. She didn't shrug him off, so he pulled her closer. She slipped her arm around him and laid her head on his shoulder.

They walked along in silence for a few minutes before Rupe drew to a halt. He eased Jayne around to face him. Her hazel eyes were shining in the approaching dusk, and something in their depths made Rupe lean down and touch his mouth to hers. He pulled back, and when she sighed and slowly blinked before parting her lips, Rupe cupped his hands around the back of her neck and slanted his mouth across hers. He had every intention of keeping the kiss light and soft, but when Jayne buried her hands in his hair and flicked her tongue inside his mouth, he lost all reason. He stepped into her, his cock thickening as he deepened the kiss.

Jayne pressed herself against his erection, but when a low, deep groan eased from his throat, she tore her mouth from his and took a step away.

"We shouldn't have done that."

"You're kidding, right?" Rupe said, his voice thick with desire. "Come on, Jayne. Let's face facts. I'm attracted to you. You're attracted to me. We're both single, consenting adults. What's the problem?"

Jayne stuck her hands in the back pockets of her shorts and began to walk back towards the car. Rupe watched her for a few seconds before jogging after her. He fell into step beside her but didn't speak. This was Jayne's issue, and she was going to have to sort through it on her own.

They drove back to London in virtual silence. As Rupe pulled into the kerb outside Jayne's apartment, she twisted in her seat.

"I'm sorry," she said, her eyes downcast. "You're right. I am attracted to you, but the timing is all wrong. You're still in a lot of trouble with the police, and I'm going through a messy divorce. This just isn't going to work."

As she made a move to get out of the car, Rupe stopped her. "That is such bollocks, Jayne," he said, ignoring the fact her eyebrows almost disappeared into her hairline at his directness. "This has nothing to do with shit timing. You're hiding behind that excuse because you're scared of commitment, of giving yourself to another man, in case he does the same thing as your husband."

Jayne shot him a furious look. "You don't know *anything* about what I'm feeling, but you're right about one thing: I will *never* allow myself to be hurt by a man again, especially one like you who sees nothing wrong in shagging married women. You need to remember that on the other end of that marriage is a *person*."

Rupe flinched. *Fuck.* When she let go, she did it in style. He ducked his head. "You're right. Not once during my fling with Nessa did her husband cross my mind. That was partly because she assured me that they didn't have a real marriage, but I'll admit I was thoughtless and selfish, and boy, am I paying for that wake-up call."

Jayne closed her eyes, and when she opened them, they'd softened. "I'm sorry. That was mean."

"No, it was factual." Rupe took her hands in his. "Look, I don't care about your past, apart from the hurt it caused. But the bad experience with Kyle has made you bury the woman you truly are so far beneath your professional exterior that I'm not sure you even know where to find her any more." He dropped her hands and turned to stare out of the windshield. "And if that's the case, then you're right—this is going nowhere."

There was the briefest pause before Jayne murmured, "Thanks for taking me today." And with that, she climbed out of the car and entered her building without giving him a backward glance.

18

Jayne spent Sunday morning thinking about the argument with Rupe. He was right: she was hiding behind Kyle's betrayal, which, in turn, was stopping her from moving on.

Every time she thought about the tightly contained passion she'd sensed in Rupe when he'd put his mouth on hers the day before, her stomach made that weird flip, like the feeling of that first dip on a rollercoaster. She'd bet Rupert Fox-Whittingham knew where all the important points were on a woman's body. No need to draw *that* man a map.

She closed her eyes as a shiver drifted over her skin, and then she shook her head. If only she weren't in the middle of a messy divorce. If only she weren't so damaged from Kyle's treachery. If only Rupe weren't her client.

Deciding that moping around would do her absolutely no good, she dressed in casual gear and went into work. No need for formal attire on the weekend.

After several hours with her head buried in case files, Jayne trudged home. Work had done its job, and she was so exhausted that her feelings for Rupe and the impossible situation they found themselves in were the last things on her mind.

But as she entered her apartment, regret, loneliness, and sorrow assailed her. Suddenly, her work, which she'd always put above everything else—even more so since Kyle's betrayal—seemed like a poor substitute for a real life.

Without invitation, her mind turned to Mike. Ten years ago, he'd been in the same position she now found herself in. He'd been trying to climb the ladder, working all hours, leaving no time for himself. Yet he'd somehow managed to have it all: a position as a top-ranking police officer, a lovely wife, and a gorgeous new baby.

She rubbed her face as an uncomfortable feeling stirred in her stomach. After analysing it, she recognised the sensation as envy. She was envious of Mike and his perfect life, and yet she could have had all that with Kyle, but she hadn't wanted to. So why was Rupe so different? She barely knew the man. Less than two weeks had passed since Darren had given her the case. *Two weeks. Jesus.*

What is wrong with me?

When her stomach rumbled, Jayne realised that she hadn't eaten all day. She opened the fridge and took out a sad little meal for one. She pricked the cellophane wrapper and put the black plastic tray in the microwave.

After toying with the food for a few minutes, barely touching it, she threw the leftovers in the waste bin and headed off to bed.

∽

SHE TOSSED and turned for what seemed like an age, but just as she was tumbling into unconsciousness, the mattress dipped beside her.

"Jayne," a warm voice murmured in her ear as a large hand

settled on her hip and pulled her close to an impossibly hard torso.

Jayne's eyes sprang open as Rupe snuggled closer. His left hand travelled over her waist, her stomach, before cupping her breast through her nightgown. Jayne repressed a groan. She should stop this before it went too far, but it had been so long since she'd felt a man's touch.

"How did you get in?" she murmured, but Rupe simply shushed her as he tugged down her nightgown and squeezed her nipple between his thumb and forefinger. Jayne arched into his hand, urging him to go harder and faster as a wave of desire crashed through her body.

Rupe eased her onto her back and slanted his mouth across hers, his tongue taking, possessing. God, this man owned her. He was proving that with his kisses alone.

As his mouth began to travel down her body, nipping, sucking, licking, Jayne clutched the bedclothes, scrunching them tightly in her hands. Her stomach clenched, and a rush of wetness pooled between her thighs. She'd been right: Rupe knew exactly where all of her pressure points were—which parts to stroke softly, which to treat roughly, which needed more attention than others. He was playing her like a finely tuned Stradivarius, and dear God, her body was singing.

Rupe settled between her legs, his day-old stubble rubbing the tender flesh between her thighs, which served to shoot her desire to the next level. He sucked hard on her clit and then used that wickedly exceptional tongue of his to plunge inside her over and over again.

"Oh, hell." Jayne cried out as her hips automatically rose off the bed. Rupe took the opportunity to cup a hand under her backside, holding her in place as his mouth worked its magic and his fingers played about with her clit.

This is so wrong, but God help me, it feels so right.

Jayne felt herself building towards an inevitable climax. She rode the wave as expertly as any experienced surfer. As she reached the crest, Rupe pressed down hard on her clit, and she crashed onto the shore.

Jayne woke covered in sweat, midorgasm. Her body twitched and pulsed as she dragged herself into full consciousness.

Oh. My. God. She'd had a dirty dream—a wet dream about Rupe, which had resulted in an orgasm.

Jayne began to laugh. In thirty-two years of life, she'd never climaxed in her sleep. If her dream turned out to be even mildly accurate…

Well, that experience had taught her one thing: she had to get Rupert Fox-Whittingham off this trumped-up murder charge. And then she needed to fuck him out of her system.

19

The following morning, Jayne gritted her teeth and picked up the phone to call Rupe. She owed it to him to make the first move, but as she dialled, heat rushed to her face as the memory of her dream came flooding back. But heat also rushed to her core as her mind picked over the vivid details of the dream.

"Good morning, Ms Seymour," Rupe said when he answered the phone.

Jayne tried to pick up on his inflection, but his voice was calm, steady, and difficult to read.

"Hi. I wondered if you were free for breakfast this morning?"

A pause. "Like a date?"

She chuckled. "No. Like a planning session. Have you received the email yet about Julie Fisher? I meant to ask yesterday."

"But you were too busy lying to yourself yesterday, weren't you, Jayne?"

She sighed. "Let's not do this."

"No, let's. Did you feel what I felt when I kissed you yesterday? Or was I imagining how perfectly we fit together? How kissing you felt like home, like where I'm supposed to be? If the kissing was that good, imagine the fucking, Jayne."

Her face heated once more, and it had only just cooled down. Could the man see inside her head?

When she didn't reply, Rupe let out a heavy breath. "Fine. Have it your way—for now. Yes, I got the email. Yes, we can meet for breakfast. I'll meet you in the coffee shop across the road from your apartment in thirty minutes, give or take, depending on traffic." He hung up without saying another word.

Jayne quickly dressed, put in a quick call to Darren to let him know she was meeting Rupe to discuss his case—not a complete lie—and stood by the window that overlooked the coffee shop. She spotted Rupe's car drawing up and stopping at the kerb. He was back to the chauffeur-driven one again, probably for convenience since it was difficult to park outside her building during rush hour. She couldn't help thinking that the limo didn't really suit him. The convertible had been much more his style: a little clichéd but hugely endearing.

She slung her bag over her shoulder, grabbed her briefcase, and darted downstairs. Despite their argument the previous evening, her stomach fluttered with butterflies at the thought of seeing him again, which was ridiculous. She wasn't sixteen and meeting her first crush. She was a grown woman—soon to be a divorcee—with a serious career. But something about Rupe made her feel skittish and ditsy.

She pushed open the door to the coffee shop and scanned the room. He was sitting at the back and had managed to grab a table by the window. He spotted her and beckoned her over. Jayne sidled past the line of people waiting for their morning caffeine fix and slipped into the chair opposite.

"I got you a latte," Rupe said. "I wasn't sure whether you wanted anything to eat."

His polite manner set her teeth on edge, but she couldn't exactly blame him. He had to be wary of her mixed signals by that point. Every time he made a move, she either threw herself at him and then backed away as fast as she could, or she refused to discuss the situation at all.

The situation? Was that what she'd compartmentalised them as? It wouldn't surprise her if she had. *Oh God.* She was all over the place. This man had her seriously rattled.

"Thanks. Coffee is fine."

Rupe frowned. "You should eat something."

The thought of food turned her stomach, because it was already full of desire. She couldn't fit anything else in. "I'll eat at the office. So you got the email?"

Rupe nodded. He pulled a folded piece of paper out of the inside pocket of his jacket and slid it across the table to her.

"It doesn't change anything," he said as Jayne unfolded it and began to scan it. "It seems Aaron did run it past me, and you'll see my reply there at the top, confirming his decision." He shrugged, although he averted his gaze, preferring instead to stare at his hands. "I honestly don't remember, but I get so many emails, and I can't be expected to recall the contents of each one."

Jayne glanced over at him. "I'm not judging," she said, but when Rupe scowled, she rushed on. "It does confirm the connection between you and Detective Fisher, though. At the very least, it calls into question his ethics, because don't tell me that he doesn't know. If he pretends it's a surprise, he's a liar."

Rupe nodded. "Are you seeing Mike Wilson today?"

"Yes, later this morning. Can I keep this?"

"Yeah. I'll forward you an electronic copy too."

Jayne downed the last of her coffee and stood. "I'll call you as soon as I've spoken to Mike." She laid a hand on his arm. "I'm sorry about yesterday. We will talk, Rupe. Just not now, okay?"

"Sure, whatever," he said almost petulantly.

Jayne ignored him. To respond would be to get into a pointless argument.

After clearing up a few things at work, she dropped Mike a

quick text to let him know she was on her way. He replied with a single word, *Good*, which ratcheted up Jayne's interest. Maybe he had some favourable news.

Mike was waiting outside his office when she arrived. He motioned her inside and pushed a cup of coffee towards her along with a plate of Danish pastries. Jayne accepted the coffee but declined the food.

"How was your weekend?" she said, remembering that he was supposed to be taking the family to the beach.

Mike chuckled. "Fine, but that's not what you're really interested in, is it, Jayne?"

Jayne smiled at the chief superintendent. "You know me too well. So have you found anything out?"

Mike nodded. "You were right about the connection regarding Fisher's sister working for one of Mr Fox-Whittingham's companies before she died."

"I know I'm right about that," Jayne said with a tinge of irritation.

Mike grinned. "Don't get tetchy. I have to check these things out for myself, Jayne. Anyway, Fisher's connection gives him a conflict of interest in the case, even if he wasn't aware."

"He's aware," Jayne said firmly.

Mike shrugged. "That may be. I've spoken to the superintendent over there this morning. We've agreed I'll interview Fisher."

"When?"

"Later this afternoon."

"I want to be there when you question him."

Mike grinned. "I had a feeling you'd say that." He rose from his desk and grabbed his jacket off the back of his chair. "Come on. I'll buy you a late lunch."

∼

JAYNE FIDGETED IN HER SEAT, her leg bouncing up and down as

she waited for Fisher to be brought into the room where his formal interview would take place. Mike had shown her to a small office where she'd be able to listen in, though she wouldn't be able to see what was going on.

After a minute or so, she heard a rustling and a door closing. Then Mike's voice, clipped and formal, said, "Sit down, Detective Fisher."

Chairs scraped along the floor, which told Jayne that Fisher had brought someone with him, as was his right during an investigation into misconduct. Her suspicions were confirmed when Mike said, "For the record, Detective Barron, you are here to observe and advise, but you cannot answer questions on behalf of Detective Fisher. Is that understood?"

A murmured, "Yes," was followed by the clearing of a throat.

"Right, let's get started." There was a rustling of papers. "Detective Fisher, my name is Detective Chief Superintendent Mike Wilson. Have you been informed of the nature of this investigation?"

"Yes," Fisher replied in a surly tone.

"Then tell me, when you brought Mr Fox-Whittingham in for questioning on Monday the third of July, did you know at that time that he was the former employer of your deceased sister?"

"Yes."

Jayne caught her breath. She'd expected more of a fight.

"Did you declare this conflict of interest to your superiors or the custody sergeant?"

"No."

"Why not?"

"Don't know."

Jayne could almost picture the sullen shrug that accompanied Fisher's reply.

"Oh, come on now, Detective Fisher. You're a seasoned officer who has been with the force for a long time. You know the procedures involving conflicts of interest. I'll ask you again. Why didn't you inform someone of your connection to Mr Fox-Whittingham?"

Fisher laughed, the sound hollow and without feeling in Jayne's ear. She shuddered.

"No comment."

"Detective Fisher," Mike said, his tone calm even though Jayne knew he'd be seething inside. "Full disclosure on your part will go a long way towards leniency in this case."

"You want full disclosure?" Fisher spat. "That pompous, rich fucker deserves everything he gets. He *killed my sister*. Let's cut to the chase, shall we, *Chief Superintendent*? What you really want to know is did I set that fucker up? The answer is yes."

Jayne sucked in a breath through her teeth and pressed the headphones closer to her ears. *Holy cow. He admitted it.*

"I couldn't believe my luck when he came in to give a statement after Vanessa Reynolds died. I volunteered to take on the case. My DI was hardly likely to refuse, given how under-resourced we are."

The monosyllabic Fisher of earlier had gone. Now, he couldn't seem to tell his story quickly enough. His gleeful tone told Jayne he had no remorse for what he'd put Rupe through.

"Baz—that's the drug pusher who fingered Whittingham—is one of my informants. He was happy to oblige."

"Let me get this absolutely clear, Detective Fisher," Mike said. "You're saying that the crucial piece of evidence against Mr Fox-Whittingham, namely that he'd bought heroin from a drug pusher the night before Mrs Reynolds died, is a fabrication?"

"Yeah." Fisher laughed. "I knew I wouldn't get away with it for long, but it was worth it to put that bastard through the wringer."

Silence filled Jayne's ear. She could picture Mike gathering his thoughts.

"Detective Fisher, I am suspending you immediately pending further investigation into your conduct in this matter. You will be on full pay until the investigation is complete. Please turn in your warrant card."

Jayne didn't need to hear any more. She dragged off the headphones and dropped them onto the desk. She closed her eyes and took a few deep breaths. Although this didn't answer the question of who'd pumped Vanessa Reynolds with enough heroin to kill her, it did at least absolve Rupe of the only evidence tying him to her death. The CPS would have to drop the charges against him.

A couple of minutes later Mike appeared, looking furious. He slammed the door behind him. "Did you listen to the lot?"

She nodded. "At least up to the point where you suspended him."

"Fucker," Mike said through clenched teeth. "As if this job isn't tough enough. Bent coppers like Fisher just make it all the harder."

Jayne rose from her chair and swept a hand down his arm. "Drink?"

"Yeah. Better make it a double."

"So what happens now?" Jayne said once they were settled in a pub not far from Kennington station with much-needed glasses of wine.

"The CPS is in the process of dropping the case against your client. The overall case is still open, though, so there's no guarantee that he wouldn't be charged in the future if the evidence points that way. After all, a woman has still died under suspicious circumstances."

"I understand," Jayne said. "Thank you, Mike. Thank you so much."

Mike shook his head. "No, thank you, Jayne, for trusting me enough to bring it to my attention." He clinked his glass against hers. "Cheers."

As she and Mike left the pub, a taxi was just dropping someone off. She said goodbye to Mike and jumped in the back. She gave the driver Rupe's address. It was time to celebrate.

20

Rupe slammed the front door when he got home after his abortive breakfast with Jayne. Maybe he needed to back right off and let Jayne come to him when she was ready, rather than constantly pushing and cajoling her. But then he might have to go days without seeing her, and that wouldn't do. Not at all.

He ignored Abi's bright chatter, instead choosing to lock himself away in his study. It was so strange: he was more concerned with his lack of progress with Jayne than the murder charge looming over his head, which was completely preposterous.

He got caught up in the vast amount of work that he'd been putting off for too long, and before he knew it, the day was drawing to a close. He heard Abi leave, although she didn't come to say goodbye, probably because she sensed his mood. He'd make sure to apologise the next time he saw her.

Five minutes later, a loud knock at the door had his heart thumping. Maybe Jayne had decided to call by. He swung open the heavy door. Outside, two suits held police identity cards in his face. *Not again.*

"Mr Fox-Whittingham. I'm Detective Chief Inspector Bailey. This is Detective Inspector Andrews. May we come in, please?"

"Come to charge me with another murder?" Rupe stood back to let the officers inside. "This one must be serious if I get the big brass. What happened to the delightful Detective Fisher?"

Both detectives ignored him, although the younger one, Andrews, smirked, and then straightened his face when Bailey glared at him. Rupe invited them to sit in the living room.

"So, gents, to what do I owe the pleasure?"

DCI Bailey cleared his throat. "Mr Fox-Whittingham, I'm here to let you know that all charges against you in relation to the death of Mrs Vanessa Reynolds have been dropped, although I would like to point out that this does not mean that you couldn't be charged again in the future."

Rupe's mouth fell open. Jayne's friend must have come through. If that was true, where the hell was Jayne? He'd have thought she'd have come to see him the minute she heard. It seemed he wasn't as important to her as he'd hoped. Somehow, that thought took the edge off his delight at the news.

"Why?" Rupe said.

Bailey recoiled in surprise. "Why?"

"Yeah. You guys were so sure I did it. What's changed?" he said, deciding that as these fuckers had wasted his time and given him several sleepless nights, he was going to make them feel a little uncomfortable.

A flush crept across Andrews's cheeks, and he swallowed hard as he fidgeted in his seat. Bailey was more successful at hiding his discomfort, although he did clear his throat once more, a sure sign that both he and Andrews had drawn the short straw in coming to give Rupe the news.

"We discovered that the eye witness wasn't reliable," Bailey said.

Rupe frowned. "What do you mean?" he said, stretching out their discomfort.

"Erm, well it seems that, erm, he'd been coerced into giving a false statement."

Rupe leaned forward in his chair, his forearms resting on his knees. "Is that so? This doesn't have anything to do with Detective Fisher, by any chance?"

Bailey paled. "I'm afraid we can't discuss internal police business, Mr Fox-Whittingham."

Rupe gave a sharp laugh. "Sure you can't. But you can charge an innocent man with murder. Throw him in the police cells for a night, drag him into court. In fact, if it hadn't have been for my brilliant lawyer and a sympathetic magistrate, I'd have spent the last two weeks at Her Majesty's pleasure."

Bailey's spine stiffened. "Please remember, Mr Fox-Whittingham, that a young woman has died. We owe it to her and her family to find out who was responsible, and if that means treading on a few toes, then so be it."

"And I'd appreciate it if *you* remember that I *knew* Mrs Reynolds. No one is sorrier than me that she is no longer here. But know this: if I find out that Fisher was behind some sort of vendetta because he blames me for the death of his sister, then I won't rest until that man pays. Do I make myself clear?"

Bailey's shoulders sagged as he realised that Rupe knew more than they had thought. He got stiffly to his feet, followed by Andrews. "Well, thank you for your time, Mr Fox-Whittingham. The CPS will be in touch with a formal notification regarding the charges being dropped."

"Thanks," Rupe muttered ungratefully. He opened the front door and watched as the officers drove away. He was about to close it when a taxi pulled up, and Jayne climbed out. Her face was flushed, her soft russet eyes shining in triumph. He gave her a hard stare, and she stopped in her tracks.

"Was that the police leaving?"

"Yes," Rupe said, his tone sharp.

"They told you, right?" she said, a frown marring her perfect features as she laid eyes on his deep scowl. "The charges are being dropped?"

"Yes, they told me," Rupe turned around and went back inside the house. Jayne must have followed because he heard the front door click shut. He wandered into the kitchen and picked up a bottle of whiskey.

"Want one?" he said as Jayne appeared at the kitchen door, her frown deeper, confusion and hurt warring for equal face time.

"I think I'd better. I thought you'd be thrilled."

"I am," he said, pouring two large measures. He pushed one across the kitchen island towards her. "But I'd rather have heard it from you before Laurel and fucking Hardy turned up here."

Jayne rested her hands low on her hips. "I only found out a short time ago. Mike said the CPS was preparing the paperwork. I didn't expect the police to get here so quickly."

"You could have called," he said, knowing he was being childish but unable to stop himself.

"I wanted to see your face, but now that I have, I wish I hadn't bothered." When he didn't reply, she let out a deep sigh. "Congratulations, Rupert. You're in the clear. Enjoy your freedom."

When she disappeared into the hallway, Rupe muttered, "You dickhead, Witters," under his breath. He ran after her and wrapped an arm around her waist as she reached for the front door. He pulled her flush against him. "I'm sorry," he murmured in her ear.

"Get off me," she gritted out.

"No." He brushed her hair over her shoulder, leaving part of her neck bare. He pressed his lips against her warm skin, and she shuddered.

"I'm warning you, Rupert," she said, pushing back against him. He hardened at the feel of her soft body and the way her backside pressed into his crotch.

"I told you, Jayne, I like it rough." His tongue traced a path from her shoulder up to her ear, and he gently sucked on her earlobe.

Jayne groaned and tilted her head farther to the side.

"I'm a free man, Jayne. There's nothing standing in the way of us being together—apart from you. What's your next excuse going to be?"

"I hate you," she said.

"Lying to yourself again, Jayne?"

He spun her around in his arms, his eyes searching hers. She broke from his gaze.

"Trust me," he said softly.

Jayne slowly lifted her chin, and for the first time, he saw raw vulnerability. And then she looked past him, over his shoulder.

"Don't hurt me," she said, her voice so low that he had to strain to hear her, even at such a close distance.

He curved his hands around her face, leaned in and kissed her, slow and languorous. His pulse kicked up a notch when she kissed him back.

"You're safe with me." He took her hand and led her upstairs.

21

Jayne's heart thundered, loud and fast, as Rupe guided her upstairs. It had taken a lot for her to give in, despite the rather cocky promises that she'd made to herself after she'd had that wet dream. Her cheeks reddened at the memory.

As Rupe pushed open the door to what she assumed was his bedroom, he frowned. "Why are you blushing?" When Jayne simply shook her head, he chuckled. "Don't tell me—you're a virgin."

"Very funny."

He trailed a fingertip down her burning cheek. "So why the flushed face?"

"Nothing," Jayne said, desperate to get him off the subject. "It's been a while, that's all."

Rupe's expression switched from teasing to serious. "If it's too soon—"

She cut him off by placing two fingers over his mouth. "Stop giving me a way out. I want this. I *need* this."

Rupe nodded as he slowly removed the pins from her hair. When it fell around her shoulders, he threaded his hands through it, feathering the strands. "You should wear your hair down more often."

"So you've said. It's too impractical."

He twisted a lock around his finger. "But very sexy."

Jayne's breath hitched in her chest. She was being seduced by a master craftsman. Rupe was unhurried in his approach as he slipped her jacket from her shoulders. He laid it over the arm of a nearby chair, which surprised her. She'd expected him to toss it on the floor and move on to the next item of clothing. Instead, he froze in place, his eyes searching her face as though looking for a sign. When she nodded almost imperceptibly, he gave a broad white-toothed smile that made her knees shake and her stomach do the most delicious backflips.

He unfastened the buttons on her blouse, taking his time with each and every one. His fingers brushed her skin, lighting her on fire, and she shivered with delight. He pushed aside the two separate parts of her blouse to reveal a dusky pink bra that was her favourite but which she never wore to work. Perhaps she'd envisaged her day ending up like this—with her standing, nearly naked, in Rupe's bedroom.

He made a sound of approval in his throat, his eyes glistening as they raked over her breasts, which peeked over the lace top of the balconette bra.

"Please tell me you're wearing matching knickers," he said, his voice low and husky.

Jayne felt her body loosen up. She'd always been a confident sexual partner, something Kyle had had trouble with. She sensed Rupe wouldn't have the same issues.

"Why don't you take my skirt off, and then you'll find out."

His eyes closed. When he reopened them, they held a hunger that took Jayne's breath away. His hands snaked around her back, and he rolled down her zipper. The skirt dropped to the floor. Jayne was thrilled she'd chosen to wear stockings, because the look on Rupe's face when his eyes fell on her matching suspender belt and thong was priceless.

"I'm not sure what I've done to deserve you, but I owe someone big time."

Jayne tilted her head to the side. "I'm not sure you've done enough to say you deserve me yet."

Rupe grinned, the lighthearted cad making a brief appearance before the serious lover returned. He took a step back, his eyes raking over her as she stood there in an outfit that was probably a fantasy for a lot of guys.

"Undress me, Jayne," he said, his voice a guttural growl.

She swiftly pulled his T-shirt over his head and unfastened his belt. With nimble fingers, she unbuttoned his jeans, and as she peeled them down his legs, his erect cock sprang free. *Jesus, he's commando. And he's enormous.* He stepped out of his jeans and kicked them to one side, his face breaking into a grin as he correctly read Jayne's surprised look.

"I prefer to let the air flow," he said, drawing a much-needed laugh from her, which broke the tension.

"You're an idiot."

He reached for her, pulling her close to his body, and with his hands in her hair, he pressed his lips to hers once more. They were searing hot. He licked inside her mouth and wrapped his tongue around hers. At the same time, he slowly began to walk backwards, pulling her along with him until he fell on the bed and she landed on top of him. Like a pair of teenagers, they began to giggle until Rupe rolled over. As she lay beneath him, his eyes grew serious, his smile draining away. What replaced that smile was a longing and a hunger so deep that it made Jayne snatch a breath. If he was even half as good as her dream, she was in for a hell of a ride.

His mouth closed over hers but didn't linger. His red-hot lips blazed a trail over her neck and across her collarbone, sinking farther south until he reached the swell of her breasts. He trailed one finger inside the lace cup of her bra, and as he brushed against her nipple, her stomach convulsed, and she hissed through her teeth.

He lowered his head, eased the cup of her bra down, and sucked her erect nipple into his warm, wet mouth. He wasn't gentle, but she didn't want gentle. She wanted hard and rough. She wanted to know, at the end of the night, that she'd been well and truly fucked.

She held his head firmly to her breast, and he picked up her cue, sucking on her nipple even harder. The sensation crossed over into pain when he bit, but *dear God,* it was oh, so good.

"Too much?" he murmured as he laved her nipple with his tongue.

Jayne shook her head. "Not enough." She felt him grin against her flesh.

"Oh, Jayne, I think you may be my perfect woman." He popped out her other boob so they were both sitting proud, supported by the underwire of her bra.

"Do you want to take it off?"

He shook his head. "I like the way they look, all bunched up like that." His hands curved around her wrists, and he held her arms on either side of her head as he sucked hard on her breasts. Rupe hadn't been joking when he said he liked it rough, but Jayne was discovering something new about herself: she liked it rough too.

He began to kiss farther down her body, but before he could delve between her legs and bring her dream to life, she put out a hand to stop him.

"Turn around," she said. "If you're going to suck me, I want to suck you."

The groan that eased from his throat was the sexiest thing Jayne had ever heard, and a fresh gush of wetness pooled between her legs. He positioned his erection in line with her mouth and hooked her leg over his shoulder. As he swept his tongue over her folds, she clenched her hand around the base of his cock and pulled him inside her mouth. Because of his size, every time he thrust in, the head of his cock hit the back of her throat, but he withdrew before her gag reflex kicked in.

His teeth grazed her clit, and then he pushed his tongue inside her. He repeated the movement, and Jayne felt her insides building. The live version was so much better than her dream.

He pinched her clit between his fingers, sending her plunging into acute pleasure. Her body clenched around his tongue, which was still buried inside her. With a jerk, his cock twitched, and he came, pouring his semen into her mouth.

As he moved away, he'd barely softened, which was just fine by her, because as good as that had been, she wanted him inside her.

He twisted around and captured her face between his hands before kissing her hard. "Fuck, you give good head."

"You're pretty good yourself," Jayne said with a smile.

"Give me five, and then I'm screwing you, so you'd better be prepared."

Jayne chuckled. "Thanks for the warning."

Rupe tilted his head to one side. "You know, Jayne, very few people surprise me, but you certainly have."

"How so?"

He shrugged. "I expected you to be more withdrawn. I thought I'd have to coax you to let go. How wrong I was."

Rupe leaned over to the cabinet beside his bed and removed a condom from an already open box. Jayne winced but clamped down on the feeling immediately. She had no right to go down that road. For God's sake, she'd only met Rupe because he'd been in bed with a woman when she'd died. Did she think he was a monk? Regardless, she filed away the stab of jealousy for examination at a later date, because it couldn't go unaddressed.

"Here," he said, passing the square foil packet to her. "I hate condoms, but I like the idea of you rolling this onto me. One thing's for sure, though—we're getting checked out, and then I'm barebacking you."

Jayne raised an eyebrow. "And what say do I get in this?"

Rupe kissed the tip of her nose. "None. Now, hurry up, because my cock is straining to be inside you."

"You are such a charmer." Jayne rolled the rubber down his erection. She expected him to assume a missionary position, but instead, he turned onto his back.

"I've fantasised for days about your hair falling all over my chest. Tonight, I'm fulfilling that dream. So, you—on top. And keep the thong on."

With a grin, she straddled his thighs. After tugging her underwear to one side, she positioned his erection at her entrance and slowly lowered herself down one inch at a time. Any faster, and her muscles wouldn't be able to expand in time. The groan that escaped her when he was fully buried inside didn't sound like her at all.

They began to move in unison, instantly finding a rhythm that usually took practice to arrive at—and even then didn't always work out. It hadn't with Kyle. They'd never quite got the tempo right, even after years of being together. But with Rupe, it was easy. He was the perfect key to her lock.

"Jesus, Jayne." Rupe gripped her hips, his fingers digging into her flesh as he controlled the movement. "Talk about fantasies coming true."

Lost in the moment, Jayne barely acknowledged that he'd spoken. A swell began to grow within her, and then, just when she thought it couldn't peak any higher, her orgasm broke. The inner muscles of her core contracted furiously, and as she collapsed onto Rupe's damp chest, she was vaguely aware of him groaning his own release.

She waited for her breathing to even out before slowly rising off his softening penis, but even with the reduced size, she winced as her body released him.

She flopped onto her back, her skin slick with sweat. A surge of emotion rose within her, and her eyes began to sting with unshed tears. *What the hell?* She wasn't the teary type, but one masterful shag with a man who clearly knew what he was doing, and she was all of a dither. She squeezed her eyes tightly shut, but when Rupe closed his hand over hers, she couldn't hold back, and a single tear ran down her cheek.

Rupe propped himself up on one elbow. "Jayne? What's the matter? Did I hurt you?"

She shook her head. A maelstrom of emotions circled within her—pleasure beyond anything she'd ever experienced, an overwhelming sadness she didn't understand, and the most frightening of all: regret. This had been a mistake. She was too broken, too emotionally inhibited to start up a new relationship right then. She'd wanted to fuck him out of her system, but that had been the wrong strategy. She was feeling things she shouldn't with a guy she barely knew. Rupe was a cad, a playboy, a hedonist. If she let him, he'd take her precious, burgeoning self-confidence and stamp all over it.

As fear and panic swept through her, Jayne shoved her boobs back into her bra, swung her legs over the side of the bed, and dragged on her skirt.

"What's going on?" Rupe said as she fastened the zipper. "Where the hell are you going?"

She turned to him, eyes glistening as she shrugged into her shirt and quickly fastened the buttons. She blinked two or three times to clear her hazy vision. "I'm sorry. This was a mistake."

She scanned the room for her shoes, eventually spotting them by the door to Rupe's bedroom. *How the hell did they end up over there?*

"What do you mean, a mistake? Jayne, for fuck's sake, talk to me."

She shoved her feet into her shoes and gave him a last glance.

"Forgive me," she said before wrenching open the door and hurtling down the stairs.

Jayne ran up Rupe's ridiculous gravel path, her shoes sinking into the driveway from hell. At the sound of gravel crunching behind, she knew Rupe was coming after her. She spilled onto the street, but there were no damn taxis. Why couldn't she catch a break? She risked a look over her shoulder. Rupe was half-dressed, shoeless, and catching up fast. Jayne put a spurt on. She was being a coward. Soon, she'd have to speak to him, but right at that moment, she didn't have the guts.

She rounded a corner at the bottom of the street, and a huge sense of relief hit her. A taxi was idling by the roadside, the orange light on the roof lit like a beacon from a lighthouse to a ship in a storm.

Jayne threw herself inside. "Go, please, just go," she shouted at the bemused taxi driver.

"Right-o, love," he said and, as Rupe made a lunge for the door, the taxi sped away.

She risked a glance out of the back window. Rupe was holding his palms in the air, a look of complete confusion on his handsome face.

Jayne twisted back around and let her tears fall.

22

Rupe balanced on a nearby lamppost and picked gravel from the soles of his feet. What the hell had just happened? He searched his mind, trying to figure out what had spooked her, but came up empty. The sex had been great. No, strike that. The sex had been out of this world, bloody fantastic, and he'd thought she felt the same. Clearly, he was wrong.

He limped back to the house and got dressed. A glance at the clock on the kitchen wall said it was too late to chase after her—even though his instincts were screaming at him to follow her and demand an explanation.

He put in a quick call to Cash to let him know the police had dropped the charges. He tried desperately to keep his voice light. If Cash suspected anything other than intense joy, he'd start to ask questions, and Rupe wasn't ready to answer them yet, not even when they came from his best friend.

He poured himself three fingers of whiskey, put on some music in the living room, and settled in, closing his eyes. She couldn't have been faking, not with the noises she'd made, the way her body had arched beneath his, and the way she'd thrown her head back when she'd been on top. He thought of how her pussy had gripped him as she came. No one was that good an actress—not even a lawyer who was used to playing up in court.

This time, she could damn well come running to him. He was done.

∼

The minute Rupe opened his eyes, he checked his phone for messages. He'd received plenty but none from the person he most wanted to hear from. He cursed. Despite his promise of the previous evening that she could come to him, he still thought she owed him an explanation for running off the way she had—and he was going to collect.

But as he grabbed his keys and his wallet, he hesitated. He needed a female point of view about what had gone on, and not from someone he'd been balls deep inside. No, he needed an honest-as-the-day-is-long woman who'd give it to him straight, even if she had a tongue as sharp as a scalpel and never apologised for cutting out your innards and then feeding them to the cat.

He needed to talk to Emmalee.

∼

Em didn't hide her look of annoyance when she found Rupe on her front step.

He ducked his head in embarrassment. "Sorry, I should have been round sooner." Then he gave her a foppish grin and threw his arms out to the side. "Ta-da."

Em stuck her right hip out to the side. "Well, well, he lives. And not only that. From what I understand, he's also not going to need me to bring packets of ciggies to prison so he doesn't end up somebody's pretty-boy fuck bunny."

Rupe pulled her into a rough hug. "Love you too, darling. Now, get the kettle on, I need your help with something."

Em extricated herself from his grasp. "You are such a dick, Rupe. Honestly, when Tal called me last night and said they'd dropped the charges, I was pleased as fuck, but I'd have preferred to hear it from you. A text, a WhatsApp message—Jesus, you could have sent me a Snapchat picture of you holding a Get Out of Jail Free card from the *Game of Thrones* version of Monopoly."

"You're right," he said, nudging her farther into her hallway.

He knew she'd relented when she let out a loud huff and turned on her heel before heading for the kitchen.

Rupe pulled out a stool at the breakfast bar and sat down. "David at work?"

"Yeah." Em filled the kettle from the tap. "You're lucky to catch me in too. I had a client cancel." She spooned instant-coffee granules into two mugs and came to sit beside him. "So what's up?"

"I need a female point of view on an... erm... situation."

"You haven't killed another one with your supreme sexual prowess, have you?"

Rupe rolled his eyes.

"Sorry," she said. "That was in poor taste."

"Nothing like that. It's to do with my lawyer."

Rupe filled Em in about the last couple of weeks. She interjected a couple of times to clarify things about Jayne, but mostly, she just listened, throwing in the odd nod or "hm." When he finished, she sat back, her keen gaze studying his face.

"You know, sometimes, I don't think you should be let out alone."

"What's that supposed to mean?"

Em shook her head. "I can't believe you're surprised this girl ran out on you." As Rupe began to speak, Em raised her hand. "I mean, for one second, look at this from her perspective. She was your lawyer, which in her head must still seem weird—sleeping with an ex-client. She's going through what sounds like a shitty divorce after the person who was supposed to love her the most betrayed her in the worst possible way. She barely knows you, and you can be pretty full-on at times. Need I go on?"

"I am not full-on."

"Yeah, right."

"But she didn't show any signs of being unhappy when I was screwing her."

Em raised her eyes heavenward. "You really don't understand women at all, do you? Here's a quick education session for you: when men sleep with women, it's physical. When women sleep with men, it's *emotional*. And often that emotion hits *after* the act, not during it."

Rupe rubbed a hand over his face. "Okay, so tell me what to do, because I can't lose her."

Em tilted her head to one side. "Wow. You're that keen?"

"You know me. I don't do relationships, but there's something about this one... something special."

Em smiled and slapped him on the arm. "I have been waiting *years* for this. Oh. My. God."

"Yeah, yeah," Rupe said, rubbing his arm where Em had struck him. "So tell me, oh wise one, how do I handle this without scaring her any more than I already have?"

Em rubbed the tips of her fingers over her lips. "You have to be less Rupert-like for a start."

"I already came to that conclusion all by myself, thanks, Em. I have been less Rupert-like."

She raised her eyes heavenward. "Sure you have. Stop with the quips, and don't even try to argue, because I know you, remember? Give her space. Be her *friend*."

Rupe pulled a face. "Does that mean no sex?"

"Yes, dickhead. The fact that she slept with you and then did a Usain Bolt tells me she thinks it was too soon. She's probably disgusted with herself. Go and see her today. Don't let the time slip by, but tell her that you understand and you won't push her.

Reassure her that you like her company and want to spend more time with her, no strings attached."

Rupe stroked his chin. "You know, Fallon, you're pretty smart."

"I know. Now, go get the girl."

~

Rupe arrived at Jayne's offices at a little after eleven. She might be in court, but he'd check there first. With Em's advice ringing in his ears, he'd refrained from buying flowers.

He took the lift up to her floor and strode down the hallway. Jayne's PA lifted her head as he got closer, a flash of surprise crossing her face.

She scrambled to her feet. "Hi, can I help you?"

Rupe cocked his head at Jayne's office door. "Is she in?"

"No. She called in sick this morning."

Rupe frowned as a sense of unease made his skin prickle. "Sick? What's wrong with her?"

"I don't know. Jayne's never sick. She called me early this morning to ask me to cancel all her appointments." She tightened her jaw, almost as though she thought she'd shared too much and was stopping any further mistakes from slipping out.

"Thanks," Rupe muttered as he spun on his heel.

"Can I give her a message?" the PA called after him. He ignored her and stepped back into the lift.

His car pulled up outside Jayne's apartment building, and he jogged up the stairs. He knocked at her door. Silence. He knocked again, and even though no sound came from beyond the apartment door, Rupe knew she was inside.

"Jayne," he called out softly. "Please let me in."

No response.

"Jayne, I know you're in there. I want to talk to you, but if you don't want to, that's fine. Just let me sit with you. I heard you're sick."

"Go away," her muffled voice bled through the door.

Rupe breathed a sigh of relief. "Come on, babe. Open up."

"I'm not your babe."

Rupe repressed a laugh as he imagined her gritting the words out through a clenched jaw that might result in a trip to the dentist.

"Yes, you are," he said. "You know how I know that?"

Another pause. "Go on, then. I'll play your stupid games. How?"

"Because I've never called a woman that before. Because that word is as special to me as you are. Because.... look, Jayne, please let me in. I don't want to have this conversation through two inches of wood."

At least thirty seconds scraped by before the lock rattled. Jayne pulled back the door and immediately turned around and flopped onto the sofa. She was swaddled in a full-length dressing gown, her hair hanging in beautiful waves over her shoulders. Rupe closed the door and sat down beside her.

She refused to look him in the eye, so he took her hand in his. Her skin felt chilly, despite the heat from the sun warming the apartment. He half expected her to tug her hand away, but she didn't.

"I went to your work. They said you were sick," he said.

She glanced at him before studying her hand in his. "I pulled a sickie," she said, chewing on her lip. "Never done that before."

Rupe chuckled. "With the amount of hours you work, Jayne, I'd say you were due."

"Couldn't face going in," she mumbled.

Rupe frowned. She was being very un-Jayne-like. She seemed almost defeated.

He gently cupped her chin and eased her around to face him. "What happened yesterday?"

She grazed her bottom lip with her teeth. "I'm sorry for

running out. It was childish and stupid and not the way I usually behave."

When no further explanation was forthcoming, he gave her a faint smile. "Look, how about I talk and you listen? That might make this a little easier."

She tucked her legs up on the couch, and his stomach clenched as a flash of leg peeked out from beneath her dressing gown before she covered herself. Em's voice rang in his mind. *No sex!*

"I know you've been hurt, Jayne. I know Kyle's betrayal of your trust has manifested itself in you closing yourself off and compartmentalising all men into fucking little shits." She managed a wan smile, and he continued. "Yet last night, I caught a glimpse of the real Jayne, didn't I? That's why you're so spooked. This controlled, closed-off impression you show the world is all a front. Underneath, you're warm, funny, generous, kind, giving—and absolutely wild in bed."

Her lips twitched, yet at the same time, she shook her head.

"I'm so sorry your husband turned out to be a bastard, but we're not all like that. I haven't exactly been a saint—far from it—but I would *never* do to a woman what your husband did to you. I know you think I'm a playboy, and until I met you, that would be an accurate assumption." He squeezed her hand. "I'm going to be honest with you, Jayne. The way you made me feel last night… I've never felt like that with any woman I've ever been with, and not just because the sex was off-the-planet fucking fantastic—that goes without saying. It's because being with you felt like where I'm supposed to be. But," he said, raising a hand as she began to speak, "I can see that you're not ready. So I have a proposal."

Jayne's brow furrowed. "What kind of a proposal?"

"Let me be your friend. And not friends with benefits—at least not yet," he added with a cheeky grin. "I like being with you. I like your company, the way we banter with each other. Let me be your shoulder to lean on. Yes, you're an independent woman, but that doesn't mean you have to do everything yourself. Depending on me doesn't weaken you. No strings, I promise."

Jayne tapped her fingers against her mouth as she scrutinised his face, no doubt looking for signs of sincerity. Or the opposite. "I could use a friend," she finally said in a quiet voice.

A surge of hope swelled within him. Emmalee Fallon was a bloody genius. He leaned in and gave her a hug, purposely keeping it light and quick. "I'm so glad."

She glanced at her watch. "I know it's early, but I really need a drink. Want one?"

"That would be lovely."

She returned with two glasses of wine. "Might as well make the most of my unexpected sick day."

He clinked their glasses together. "To friendship."

Jayne nodded and took a sip. She placed her glass on the table next to her and pinched her nose between her thumb and forefinger. "I'm so tired. I need a break."

"Then take one."

She shook her head. "My caseload is off the charts."

"You'll be of no use to anyone if you burn out, Jayne. Delegate. Shift a few cases to others within your firm, or get in some temporary help."

She frowned slightly as she considered his suggestions. "I guess I could. Might take me a few weeks to sort, but..." She smiled brightly. "You know what? I'm going to do it." She rubbed her hands together. "Now, where should I go?"

Rupe smiled. "Ah, now, I might be able to help you out with that."

23

"Oh, Rupe, it's gorgeous."

Jayne took Rupe's hand as he helped her aboard his boat. He'd done nothing but talk about his pride and joy for the last four weeks, ever since Jayne had agreed to his offer of a holiday—ten days in which Rupe had promised her the best time of her life, with no strings whatsoever.

He was making good on that promise already.

"She is amazing, isn't she?" he said fondly as his hand trailed along the polished wooden rail at the stern.

Like an excited little boy, Rupe showed her around. The boat was huge, though several surrounding yachts moored in Miami's harbour dwarfed it. Seriously, Rupe's was plenty big enough. She couldn't imagine what anyone would do with even more space.

"So when do we set sail?" she said as they emerged on deck once more.

"Tomorrow. It would have been better if you'd managed to take a little more time off work, but we can still see two or three islands on the western side of the Caribbean in the time we have."

An excited thrill ran through her, not just because of the upcoming much-needed holiday but because she was spending it with Rupe. He'd been true to his word over the last four weeks. He hadn't laid a finger on her, he'd made sure she'd had downtime, and he'd stopped her from working herself to death. He'd even managed to persuade her to accept the latest counteroffer from Kyle, which, for some strange reason, had been entirely reasonable. As Rupe had pointed out, accepting it would mean she could finally put her marriage behind her and move on.

Move on to Rupe perhaps?

She pushed the thought aside, one that had been regularly nudging her in the weeks since Rupe had backed off after their one night together. He'd read her correctly: a friend had been exactly what she'd needed at the time. But now she wasn't so sure. Every time he took her hand or inadvertently brushed past her, her stomach would clench, and a delicious shiver would creep up her spine.

"So what have you got planned for tonight?"

Rupe made a wry face. "Don't kill me, but I thought you wouldn't mind if we met up with Cash and Tally for dinner."

Jayne tilted her head to one side. "You're taking me to meet your friends?"

Rupe slung an arm around her shoulder. It had the casual feel of friendship. Even so, Jayne couldn't help a swarm of butterflies from setting up camp in her stomach.

"Well, you're a friend of mine too. Why wouldn't I?"

She grinned. "Then I'd love to meet them. How come they're in Miami?"

Rupe chuckled. "Tally dragged Cash and the kids to Disney World—under extreme duress, I might add. But Cash has never been able to say no to Tally."

"Disney World not his thing?"

"Not even close, which is why they're here now. Cash committed to one week in the fun capital but only if they could then spend a few days here. Miami's much more his vibe. Elegant restaurants and stylish clubs rather than screaming kids, pushy parents, and endless queues."

Jayne laughed. "I'm looking forward to meeting them already."

"Well, be prepared, 'cause I'm going to rip the shit out of Cash for caving. Honestly, I swear if Tally asked him to strip naked and run down Miami Beach with his arse on fire, he'd do it."

She laughed again. "Should make for a fun night."

∽

JAYNE BIT down on her nerves as she and Rupe waited at the restaurant for Cash and Tally to arrive. She had no idea why her stomach was churning. She wasn't normally bothered by meeting new people. In her line of work, she had to do it all the time. But something about how important these two people were to Rupe, and how she'd translated that into desperately needing them to approve of her, meant she was much edgier than normal.

"There they are," Rupe said, waving his arms in the air. Jayne followed his gaze and had to swallow her surprise. She didn't know what she'd expected, but coming towards them was possibly the most attractive couple she'd ever seen. Cash was tall and broad shouldered but lean rather than heavily muscled. He was extremely handsome and perfectly matched by Tally. She had waist-length chestnut-coloured hair that fell in waves over her shoulders, piercing navy-blue eyes, skin like porcelain, and the most amazing prominent cheekbones. And her body... what Jayne wouldn't have given for some of Tally's curves.

Cash and Rupe clapped each other on the back while Tally smiled and stuck out her hand.

"You must be Jayne. We've heard so much about you."

"Please don't believe everything he says," Jayne said, cocking her head at Rupe.

"I heard that," Rupe said, while Tally chuckled.

"Good to finally meet you, Jayne," Cash said.

"Likewise," Jayne said as they took their seats.

Cash and Rupe immediately began to take the piss out of one other.

Tally rolled her eyes. "They're like this every time they get together. We may as well be part of the furniture."

Cash broke off from joking around with Rupe and snaked an arm around her shoulders. He kissed her temple. "Sweetness, you know you're the centre of my world."

His expression as he looked at his wife was one of reverence, adoration, and intense love. Jayne could barely tear her eyes away as she watched them silently converse. A connection like that between two people was so rare.

"So, Jayne," Tally said when Cash began speaking with Rupe again. "I hear Rupe is taking you on a whistle-stop tour of the Caribbean."

"Yes. It's a shame I can't get more time off work, but fighting couples await."

Tally laughed. "I can't imagine how difficult your job must be. I'm just glad Rupe had you in his corner—that's all I can say."

Rupe rose from his chair and leaned across the table. He picked up Tally's hand and kissed it. "Thank you, darling."

Jayne could have sworn she heard a low growl coming from Cash.

Rupe chuckled as he dropped Tally's hand and sat back down. "Seven years, dickhead, and you still get jealous."

"Seven years, and you still don't learn."

Rupe laughed as Tally's eyes cut to Cash. "Will you two behave, please?"

As the evening wore on, Jayne began to relax. Tally was one of the most genuine women she'd ever met. There wasn't an ounce of bitchiness in her, and her obvious love for Rupe made a twinge of envy pinch at Jayne's gut. She had friends, of course, but nothing on the scale of the connection between Rupe and Cash, and Tally seemed to be the ship that anchored them.

When coffee was served at the end of the meal, Tally got to her feet. "Just off to the ladies'," she said, giving Jayne a clear indication to follow her.

Jayne slung her bag over her shoulder, more than a little curious about what Tally wanted with her, although it wasn't very unusual for women to go to the bathroom in pairs.

"Rupe seems to like you very much." Tally removed a lipstick from her bag and began to apply a thin layer. She dabbed her lips with a tissue. "So what about you? How do you feel about him?"

Jayne held back a look of surprise at Tally's direct approach. "I'm not sure that's any of your business," she said, making sure she softened her words with a smile.

Tally tilted her head to the side. "I understand that you're going through a nasty divorce."

Jayne's eyes widened. "Does Rupe tell you and Cash everything?"

"Pretty much." Tally shrugged. "Look, I'll lay my cards on the table. Rupe is one of the most important people in my life. I love him like the brother I never had. He's a good person, a really good person, but beneath all his joviality lies a heart that would be easy to crush."

Jayne straightened her spine. "And you think I'm going to do that?"

"I didn't say that, but I know Rupe extremely well. I can tell by the way he looks at you that he's falling hard and fast. If you don't feel the same way, then please, leave him alone before he gets seriously hurt."

Incredulous, Jayne stared at Tally. "Wow… you're warning me off?"

"No. I'm asking you to search deep within your heart and figure out, bloody quick, whether Rupe could be the one for you, because I'm telling you now, he thinks you're the one for him."

A fluttering set up in Jayne's belly and wouldn't quit. "Has he said that?"

Tally shook her head. "Like I said, I know Rupe probably better than he knows himself. Please don't hurt him."

Tally's last words came out as a plea, and Jayne expelled a soft breath. "Look, I'll level with you. I don't know where this thing with Rupe is going. I've had my fingers burned, and I'm not in a rush to stick them back in the fire again. He's good company, and I really enjoy being with him, but six weeks is no length of time to make lifelong commitments."

"Six weeks is long enough for some," Tally said, almost to herself.

Jayne smiled softly. "I'm not you, and Rupe isn't Cash."

Tally grinned. "Fair point."

"You're lucky you found your soulmate, but you have to remember, I already thought I'd found mine." She laughed. "Although, looking back, I think I was more in love with the idea of being in love."

"I'm really sorry. About your husband, I mean. That's an awful thing to happen, and with your best friend. Urgh. What a bitch."

Jayne chuckled. "Wow, he really does tell you everything."

Tally clapped a hand over her mouth. "Oh, God, I'm sorry."

"Don't be. It's fine." Jayne had a final glance in the mirror. "We'd better get back before they send out a search party."

When Jayne slipped into her seat beside Rupe, he gave her a quizzical look. She smiled reassuringly and rubbed his arm. "Well, I don't know about you lot, but I'm exhausted after the long flight today."

Rupe glanced at his watch. "I'm not surprised. It's four in the morning back home. Want to go?"

"Yes, please."

As the four of them said their goodbyes with promises of a meetup when they were all back in England, Rupe slipped an arm around Jayne's waist. She probably should have shrugged him off—she didn't want him to get any mixed signals—but she was just too damned tired. She leaned her head on his shoulder as their driver took them back to the boat.

"I could get used to this," she murmured. "Great food, good company, chauffeur-driven cars."

Rupe gently kissed the top of her head. "I'm glad you liked my friends."

"I really did." Her eyes began to droop. "They're lovely people."

The car coming to a stop jolted her from sleep. Rupe walked her to her stateroom, and as she bid him goodnight, he hesitated and held her eye for a moment, but he only said, "Night, Jayne. Sleep well."

As he headed to his own stateroom, she watched his retreating back with a mixture of longing and regret. Putting her mixed feelings down to jet lag, she entered her room and promptly fell asleep.

24

Jayne dropped her beach bag on the floor and sank into the nearest chair. "I'm exhausted."

Rupe sat down opposite her. "Good day, though?"

She nodded. "Grand Turk was beautiful. I'm sorry to be leaving it behind."

"I wish we had longer too, but it's a three-day sail back to Miami, so we have to set off tonight if we're going to make our flight home. Hopefully, next time you'll be able to get more time off work."

A shiver of delight crept up Jayne's spine. *Next time.* The last few days spent on Rupe's boat had been just the tonic she'd needed. She'd been pampered by his fabulous staff, not to mention that Rupe himself had made sure that she got whatever she wanted.

"Thank you for persuading me to come. It was exactly what I needed, although I still don't understand how doing virtually nothing is so tiring."

"It's your mind's way of forcing you to rest," Rupe said as his phone rang. He dug it out of his pocket and answered it with a frown. "What's up, Aaron?" After listening for a few seconds, he nodded. "Give me five minutes." He hung up. "Can you entertain yourself for an hour? Something has come up that I need to take care of."

"Of course," Jayne said. "Go do what you need to."

"If I'm not out in an hour, come and get me. I'll be in my study."

Jayne wandered to the bow of the boat and stared at the twinkling lights of Grand Turk harbour. The waves lapped against the sides, and the warm Caribbean breeze blew her hair around her face. She'd had an amazing time during the past few days, and even though they still had three days of sailing ahead of them, melancholy swept over her. All too soon, she'd be back at work, and the responsibility of her job would once more weigh heavily upon her. Something had to give. She couldn't carry on using work as a crutch to avoid facing up to her real life, as complicated as it was.

The minutes scraped by, and as soon as the hour was up, Jayne went in search of Rupe. She found him frowning at his laptop, intense concentration making him squint at the screen.

"Almost done?" she said.

He lifted his head and smiled. "Five minutes?"

"Sure." She turned to leave.

"Stay," Rupe said, pointing at a chair opposite his desk. "I really have almost finished."

"Okay." She sat down and looked around. Screens lined one wall. Shelves full of books on software and coding lined another. A couple of printers sat atop a low mahogany table. Notebooks filled with Rupe's black scrawl lay open on his desk. "You really have got the whole setup going on here, haven't you?"

"Yep. I guess you could call this the head office for my company. At least, it's where I work most of the time."

A knot formed in her stomach. Even if she could allow herself to trust again, what sort of relationship would she and Rupe have if he spent most of his time on this boat and she was locked away in an office block in London? She pushed the errant thought aside. It was all moot anyway.

"So what are you working on—the next 'Call of Duty'?"

He stopped tapping on his computer and closed the lid. "It's a pet project, actually, but one I'm really passionate about. I can't say much as it's all a bit hush-hush, but it's basically an app that allows people to be tracked."

Jayne narrowed her eyes. "That sounds like a terrible invasion of privacy."

Rupe nodded. "You're right, but that in itself isn't new. Tracking software exists already. But what I'm doing is a little different, and trust me, I plan to use it as a force for good. If my partner and I can iron out the glitches, it'll be a great tool for the security services to use. That's the eventual plan. Free of charge to the right agencies, of course."

"Very philanthropic," Jayne murmured.

Rupe chuckled. "It might look as if I treat everything like a joke, but I do have some depth." He stood and walked around to her side of the desk. He held out his hand. "Come on, let's eat. I'm starving."

As she took it, a fluttering set off in her abdomen. *I'm starving too. And not for food.*

25

Jayne stretched her arms overhead as she languished on the soft, thick-piled sunbed on the top deck of Rupe's boat. All around, the deep-blue waters of the Caribbean gently rocked her, and above, the sun beat down as it had for the past nine days. As it dipped lower in the sky, the heat began to recede.

"I can't believe we'll be docking in Miami tomorrow and then flying home," she said as one of Rupe's deckhands topped up her mojito.

Rupe lazily turned on to his side, his deeply tanned body making his abs even more pronounced. *For God's sake, stop it, Jayne.* Ever since they'd left Turks and Caicos, she'd found it harder and harder to stop her fingers from reaching out and exploring every ridge, every muscle.

The more time they'd spent together, the less she wanted to be just friends. That was what he'd offered, and that was what she'd accepted. A deal had been struck. Yet all she wanted was to add a codicil to their unwritten contract—something along the lines of "Screw *friends*. Just screw."

She repressed a giggle. She'd definitely changed these last

few days. The heavy weight she'd carried on her shoulders from the pressure of her job and the deep hurt from Kyle's betrayal had been blown away on the warm Caribbean breeze. Maybe it was because she'd finally signed the divorce papers—or maybe it was the sun and the sea, the good food and good wine.

Or maybe it was being with Rupe.

"You know, for a blonde, you tan well, Janey," he said, his eyes half-closed as he looked at her.

"Janey?" she raised an eyebrow.

"Yeah." Rupe raised himself up on an elbow. "That name suits you better out here. Once we get back to London, you'll reassume the serious-lawyer armour plating, and it'll be back to 'anything but' plain old Jayne."

Jayne rolled her eyes even though she'd been having the same thoughts herself not one minute earlier. She pushed herself upright and took a sip of her mojito.

"Isn't plain old Jayne good enough for you any more, buddy?" she said with a grin.

"I said *anything but* plain old Jayne. And if I'm honest, I'll take you any way I can get you." His face grew serious. "It's been good to see you let your hair down and relax. It suits you." He rolled on to his back and laced his arms behind his head as he closed his eyes against the bright sun.

An uncomfortable feeling stirred in Jayne's chest. The conversation had taken a turn in the direction she wanted to go but was scared to tread. Deciding she needed to lighten the atmosphere, she scooped an ice cube out of her glass and dropped it on his belly. He yelped and leaped to his feet, and Jayne did the same. She ran around the other side of the pool, but Rupe was too quick, and before she could plead her case, he picked her up and threw her into the water.

Jayne came up choking and spluttering. She pushed wet hair off her face and pointed at Rupe, who was doubled over with laughter at the side of the pool.

"You are a dead man," she said.

He laughed harder and threw his arms out to the side. "Come and get me if you think you're tough enough."

Jayne swam to the side and climbed out of the water. She expected Rupe to run, but instead, he gathered her in his arms and jumped back into the pool.

When the pair of them surfaced, Jayne shoved him hard in the shoulder. "You're an idiot."

Rupe grinned inanely at her. "But a fun idiot."

"That's debatable," Jayne muttered.

He laughed, turned away from her, and began to swim lengths of the pool. Jayne leaned against the side and watched as his lean, lithe body cut through the water. *You're on dangerous ground, Jayne.* Her feelings were changing, deepening. This was no longer about great sex, although just how amazing the sex had been the one time they'd slept together constantly drifted into her mind and made her stomach clench with need. Was she ready? Could she trust her patched-up heart with this man? Therein lay the problem, because she just didn't know.

After an early dinner, Jayne made a lame excuse about too much sun and headed off to her stateroom. She took a quick shower and changed for bed. As she lay on her back, staring up at the ceiling, her mind wouldn't stop whirring. She closed her eyes, but the image of Rupe's tanned, tightly honed body kept playing on a loop behind her lids.

She pushed herself upright and turned on the lamp beside the bed. Her iPad called to her, and despite promising herself a full ten days off, she opened her email account. A few things had blown up at work. Jayne scanned for the most pressing ones and answered them, even though Darren would most likely give her a telling-off when he logged on in the morning.

What should I do now? She picked up a book, but after realising she'd flicked through several pages without being able to recall one single word, she put it back down.

If she went to Rupe, what was the worst thing that could happen?

He could reject her—unlikely, given his previous comments—or he might welcome her with open arms and they could spend the night exploring every inch of each other's bodies.

But what if she freaked out like last time? On the yacht, there was nowhere to run to. She couldn't exactly dive overboard and swim for shore. *God, this is so frustrating.*

She covered her face with her hands and rubbed hard. She was thirty-two years old and procrastinating over a bloody man. She wanted him. There, she'd said it. She wanted him more than any other man she'd ever slept with. Not that she'd been with a whole lot. Five, if she counted that one ill-fated night with Rupe. It wasn't as if she had a hundred men to compare him to, but still... the reactions, sensations, and noises he'd drawn from her were all new experiences. She'd always believed movie sex, or the sex found in romance novels, was just make-believe. But Rupe had demonstrated, with significant expertise, that it was possible to experience that kind of sex in real life—with the right man.

Oh, fuck it.

Jayne climbed off the bed and made for the door, but as she passed the floor-to-ceiling mirror, she stopped. If she was going to do this, then she was all-in. She grabbed the hem of her nightgown and pulled it over her head. She crossed over to the chest of drawers and opened the top one. Nestled between her everyday underwear was the set she'd been wearing when they'd slept together for the first time. *The only time.*

She donned the lingerie and stood in front of the mirror once more. Her tan made the outfit look even sexier than the last time, although she wished she had a bit more up top. Still, Rupe hadn't seemed to care, if memory served her right.

She opened the door to her stateroom and peeked into the corridor. Silence. There was a slight chance that she could bump into a member of staff, which would be highly embarrassing, but the risk was small, and Rupe's room was less than forty feet away.

Holy hell, I'm doing this.

Jayne dashed down the corridor and knocked on Rupe's door. She heard a scuffle from within before Rupe opened it.

"What the fu—"

Jayne cut off Rupe's exclamation with her mouth. She hooked her legs around his waist, her arms around his neck. Pulling back, she fixed a gaze on his startled expression.

"I'm ready," she said.

26

Rupe eased Jayne's legs to the floor. He hardened so quickly that his cock almost punched a hole in his sweatpants. He buried his hands in her hair and studied her face.

"Are you sure?" he said, hoping like fuck she didn't say no and leg it again, because his right arm couldn't take much more of a beating. His cock, on the other hand...

"Yes. I'm sorry it's taken me so long, but I want you. I want *this*." She swung her hand between them.

Rupe groaned as he caught her mouth. Jayne kissed him back, her tongue tangling with his. Jayne was no passive participant. She was a lady who liked to take her turn at leading, and right then, Rupe was so stunned by the turn of events that he happily acceded.

She leaned into him, pushing him towards the bed until the back of his knees hit the mattress. He sat down as Jayne straddled him, wearing the stunningly hot lingerie from the last time. He briefly wondered if she'd chosen it on purpose to remind him of their first time together.

He closed his eyes as her hands explored his chest. The touch of her fingertips against his burning skin was heavenly. She gently pressed her palms against his shoulders, and he lay down on the bed as she straddled him once more.

"See these?" She scraped a red-painted nail over his abdomen. "I want to lick every single muscle."

Rupe reached behind his head and gripped the bed frame. "I'm not stopping you."

Jayne bent over, and he inhaled a sharp breath as the tip of her tongue traced his abs. He hadn't thought his cock could get any stiffer, but it seemed he didn't know his body as well as he'd thought. The damn thing might as well have had a steel rod at its core. She began to make soft noises at the back of her throat that sounded like appreciation. Dear God, she was going to be the death of him.

With his abs still damp from the attention of her tongue, Jayne crawled up his body until her mouth was level with his, but she didn't kiss him. She simply stared into his eyes, and as she did, a warmth spread through his veins because Jayne's eyes held something deeper than lust.

"Will you do something for me?" Rupe said, his voice low and husky.

"Within reason," she said with an amused grin.

He smiled. "Strip."

She sat up and pointed at her lingerie. "You want these off?"

"Yeah," he groaned.

Jayne climbed off the bed and nodded at his pants. "You first."

Rupe yanked off the sweats. His erection sprang free, and as he lay back down, it stretched towards his midriff. When Jayne licked her lips, he almost came.

"Stroke," she said, nodding at his cock as she slipped her garter belt down those impossibly long legs.

"Holy hell." Rupe took hold of his erection and began to rub. He'd been with a lot of women who didn't shy away from intimacy, but Jayne's sexual confidence was off the freaking charts, and he *loved* it.

With his eyes following her every move, he began to pump harder as she removed her lingerie one piece at a time. He swore she was taking her time on purpose. "I'm going to come if you don't get a move on," he said through a clenched jaw as his balls tightened.

Jayne shimmied out of her thong, the last piece of her underwear, and straddled him once more. "You wanted me to strip. The least I can do is give you a show."

In a flash, Rupe flipped her onto her back. She giggled, but he cut off her laughter with his mouth. She'd been in charge until that moment, but no longer. He gripped her chin, holding her head in place as he kissed her, while his other hand brushed her waist and moved over her hip before settling between her legs. As his fingers sought her wet heat, he let out a low moan. She wasn't just wet—she was soaking. He slid two fingers inside her, crooking them slightly until he found what he was looking for. Jayne arched her back and tore her mouth from his, incoherent mumblings falling from her lips.

As his thumb found the tight nub at the apex of her thighs, touching wasn't enough. He wanted to taste, to lick, to suck. His lips found her hard nipples, and he pulled each one, in turn, into his mouth. He slowly worked his way down her body and parted her thighs with his hands. With one large palm holding each of her legs wide apart, Rupe buried his head between them.

"Oh God." Jayne bunched the sheets in closed fists. She didn't take long. As she climaxed, she tried to ram her legs together, but he was having none of that. He pressed harder on her thighs and drew her clit into his mouth.

"It burns," she muttered. "Too much."

With a final sweep of his tongue over her slit, he crawled up her body. He reached for the drawer beside his bed and quickly located a condom. After sliding it down his length, he thrust hard, filling her in one sharp movement. Jayne cried out. He was about to hold still in case he'd hurt her, but she wrapped her legs around his waist, dug her nails into his backside, and tilted up her pelvis to greet him.

He kissed her, but as his thrusts became more urgent, he couldn't keep their lips locked. Instead, he looked into her eyes. That was his undoing. An almost violent orgasm shot from the head of his cock. His vision blurred, white dots dancing in front of his eyes.

His head fell onto her shoulder as he waited for his cock to stop pulsating. He let his weight fall on Jayne for the briefest of moments before he rolled to the side. "Please don't go."

She turned on her side and folded both hands beneath her cheek. "I'm not going anywhere."

∼

Jayne was quiet on the way to the airport, but Rupe guessed it was more to do with end-of-holiday blues than the fact that they'd spent a large proportion of the previous night and that morning exploring each other. She was gazing out of the window as the high-rises of downtown Miami swept past.

Rupe covered her hand with his. "Doing okay there, Janey?"

She twisted her head. "It's going to be tough to go back to the way things were."

A bolt of anxiety shot through his bloodstream. "What do you mean?" he said more sharply than he'd intended, which drew a raised eyebrow from her.

"Easy, tiger," she said with a grin. "I didn't mean you and me. I meant work, routine, London smog, instead of all this." She glanced out of the window once more, a soft sigh escaping her lips. "And let's face it, you'll have to go back to work soon, which will make seeing each other a little tricky."

Confused, he frowned. And then he remembered. She was

thinking about the conversation they'd had a few days ago when he'd told her that he tended to work from his boat.

"Jayne," he said softly. "Look at me." She slowly turned her head, and Rupe leaned towards her until their foreheads were touching. "I think it's time I stopped moving around. And London isn't so bad, although the weather is shit. We'd need to take quite a few holidays to make sure I get enough vitamin D."

A smile spread across her face, and she unclipped her seatbelt and straddled his legs. Her hands curved around his neck, and she kissed him—gently at first, but as he trailed the tip of his tongue across her bottom lip, she deepened the kiss. Oh, man, he loved it when she took charge. But they weren't far from the airport. He would have preferred to start something when they were airborne and tucked away in the bedroom on his plane.

He curved his hands around her face and eased her back. "One hour until we're in the air. Then you're mine."

Jayne gave him a look of reprimand. "That sounds remarkably like a statement of ownership. You picked the wrong girl for that."

Rupe grinned as he feathered his hands up and down her sides. "Oh, I don't know," he said, caressing her nose with his. "I think the tigress can be tamed with the right approach."

She poked him hard in the ribs before twisting out of his arms. "I thought you liked my bite."

"Oh, babe, I do. But I have the feeling I still need to work on making sure that bite only ever sinks into *my* flesh."

Jayne threw back her head and laughed. "In that case, get to work, mister."

27

Jayne couldn't raise a smile when she walked into work the day after she and Rupe landed back in the UK. She was tired, grumpy as hell, jet-lagged, and already missing the man who had become far too important to her in a short space of time.

It had crossed her mind at least ten times in the last twenty-four hours that their relationship was moving too fast, but then she'd think about not being with him, and a pang would spread through her chest.

She hadn't seen him since he'd dropped her off at her apartment the previous morning, and she missed him, which, when she thought about it, was bloody stupid. She was a grown woman, not a teenager. *I can manage on my own quite well, thank you very much.* Oh, but she ached for him. His absence had caused a great big hole to open up in her chest, and although she'd try to keep busy, she doubted work would fill it.

As she swept down the corridor, Donna rose from her desk, wearing a bright smile and holding a cup of coffee in an outstretched hand.

"It's so great to have you back," she said as Jayne took the paper cup from her. "You look amazing."

"I feel like shit." Jayne nudged open her office door with her hip. "Jet lag is a bitch."

Chuckling, Donna followed her inside. "Well, you've got a fabulous tan. Did you have a good time?"

Jayne pointed at the chair opposite her desk, as she slid into her own behind it. "Lovely, thank you. Now, sit down and tell me what's been going on around here," she said, refusing to spill her guts about her holiday. Donna was great at her job, but she was also the head of gossip central, not just where Jayne worked but at several other law firms too. The law community was small and tight-knit.

Donna filled her in on the past ten days' activities, and together, they went through Jayne's calendar for the rest of the week. Thank God it was already Wednesday and she had a short week. That thought caught her off guard. On the odd occasion that she'd taken a holiday with Kyle, she'd always been chomping at the bit to get back to the office, regularly working the next several weekends to catch up. But while Donna droned on, Jayne tuned her out, her mind turning to the fit-as-all-hell billionaire she'd spent the last ten days with instead.

After she finally managed to shoo her assistant out of her office, Jayne gritted her teeth, put her head down, and got to work. Every now and then, she'd reach for her phone, make sure it wasn't on silent, and then check to see if Rupe had texted her. When he hadn't, she would swallow her disappointment and go back to her caseload.

At the end of an interminably long day—made worse because of an argument with a client who seemed to think he knew better than she did—Jayne made her way to the tube. Her feet were killing her. After ten days in flip-flops and flats, her corns did not appreciate being crammed into three-inch heels.

She picked up her post and took the lift upstairs. The second she set foot in her apartment, she kicked off her shoes. After grabbing a juice from the fridge, she slumped onto the sofa and let her head fall back, her eyes closing of their own accord. She'd known the first day back would be difficult, but as the last bit of energy drained from her, she began to wonder where her mojo had gone.

First-day-back-at-work blues, that's all.

Jayne forced her eyes open and flicked through the post. *Junk, bills, more junk.* And then her tiredness was forgotten. At the bottom of the pile was a letter from her divorce lawyer. With shaking hands, she ripped open the envelope. As she scanned the letter, a sense of elation mingled with melancholy swept through her. The application for the decree nisi had been filed with the court. Although glad to be finally rid of the cheating bastard, she couldn't help feeling a sense of loss at the time wasted. Seven years of her life spent on someone who had turned out to be the epitome of everything she abhorred. In three months, she'd have to tick the "divorced" box when forms asked for "marital status."

She tossed the letter onto the coffee table and rose from the couch. Her stomach rumbled, but the thought of food wasn't as appealing as a shower. She wanted to wash away the remnants of this crappy day. And Rupe *still* hadn't called or texted her. But then, she hadn't contacted him either.

What if, now that they were home, he'd changed his mind and decided that putting down roots in London wasn't what he wanted after all?

Goddammit. She hated the uncertainty of new relationships—the way the mind played tricks, constantly throwing out multiple *what-if*s. She hated the way that her confidence ebbed, making her question absolutely everything.

She stripped off her clothes and stepped into the shower. Turning the temperature right up, she stood under the punishing spray without moving, her head tipped forward as the water cascaded over her neck and down her back. After a few minutes, she began to feel human again as both doubt and grime disappeared down the drain.

She shrugged into a dressing gown and swaddled her hair in a towel. Digging her phone out of her bag, she went to call Rupe and then chickened out. A text would seem more casual, less needy.

She wrote and deleted several messages before deciding on something light and breezy: *Hope your jet lag isn't as bad as mine.*

She added a smiley on the end. Maybe she should have ended it with a kiss. No, if she wanted to keep it casual, an emoji worked better. *Dear God, I'm getting on my own nerves. Get a grip, Jayne.*

She tossed her phone on the couch and went to dry her hair. When she returned half an hour later, she reached for it, her heart thundering as she checked out the screen. Two texts.

She opened the first: *I missed you today.*

And the second: *I'm coming over.*

Both texts had been sent one minute after hers. She jumped at a rap on the door, and her pulse jolted.

"Hang on," she called out as she looked in the mirror and checked herself out. No time to put any makeup on. She tucked her hair behind her ears and strode across her apartment.

She drew to a halt in front of the door and took a deep breath. "Hi—"

Rupe cut her off as he curved his hands around her neck and kissed her. He leaned his body into hers, forcing her to walk backwards. She heard the door slam. When they broke apart, a ghost of a smile graced his lips, but it was eclipsed by the hunger in his eyes.

"I swear today lasted about a hundred hours." He bent to peck her lips once more.

"At least you could sleep off your jet lag. I had to work."

"Oh, my poor baby." He slipped his arms around her waist. "Have you eaten?"

"Not yet."

"Why don't I order something, and then you can tell me all about your day?"

"Sounds perfect." She twisted out of his arms and removed a bunch of take-out menus from her kitchen drawer. "What do you fancy?"

"Apart from you?"

She gave him a stern look. "To eat."

Rupe chuckled. "Same answer."

She tossed the menus at him. He managed to catch most, but a couple of them fluttered to the floor. "You are such an idiot," she said with a scowl, which deepened when he laughed harder.

He picked up the fallen menus from the floor and flicked through them. "Jamaican jerk chicken it is, then," he said, which made her laugh.

Jayne poured a couple of glasses of wine as her phone rang. Her eyes widened when she saw who was calling. "Hey, Mike," she said, glancing at her watch and then at Rupe, who was wearing a puzzled look. "Is everything okay? It's pretty late."

"Yeah, sorry, Jayne," Mike said. "I was wondering if you could swing by my office in the morning."

"What for?"

"I have some news on the Vanessa Roberts death that you might be interested in."

Jayne stood up straight. "Oh yeah? Have you found out what happened to her?" She mouthed "Vanessa" at Rupe, who immediately joined her in the kitchen. She put the phone on speaker, and set it down on the kitchen counter.

"Look, it's a bit difficult over the phone. Face-to-face would be better."

She shared a look with Rupe. "You've really piqued my interest. Any reason I can't pop over now?"

"Yes, Jayne, there is. I have a wife and a daughter to get home to. Come and see me at nine tomorrow morning. And see if you can get hold of Rupert Fox-Whittingham. He should hear this too."

Jayne winked at Rupe and placed a finger over his lips. "We'll be there."

~

THE FOLLOWING MORNING, Jayne and Rupe were escorted to Mike's office, their curiosity off the charts. They'd stayed up all night running scenarios, which might have been a useless waste of time but managed to keep them sane while they waited for dawn to break.

Mike's PA told them to wait as he was on a call. She had a scowl for Jayne and a coy smile for Rupe. Jayne paced the hallway, whereas Rupe lounged in a chair, his legs splayed wide, hands laced behind his head. Honestly, the man was so laid-back, but instead of his demeanour having a calming mirrored effect on Jayne, she found her blood pressure rising.

Mike's door opened, and he beckoned to them. After brief introductions were made, he motioned for them to sit. "I'm sorry if I was a bit cloak-and-dagger last night. I wanted to make sure I could get you both to come here as soon as possible, before you hear this somewhere else."

Jayne leaned forward, sliding her chair closer to Mike's desk. "Hear what?"

As Mike rested his arms on his desk, the light from the window fell on his face, and Jayne couldn't help thinking how tired he looked. The skin beneath his eyes was dark and bruised, the lines around his mouth pronounced.

"There's been a development in the Vanessa Roberts case." He pinched the bridge of his nose. "I barely know where to start."

Jayne began to fidget in her chair. Rupe put a hand on her knee to still her. Mike spotted the affectionate touch, and his eyes widened.

"Spit it out, Mike," Jayne said. "The suspense is killing me."

Mike blew out a breath. "We've charged the husband with conspiracy to commit murder."

Rupe hissed a breath as Jayne fixed Mike with a hard stare. "So it *was* the husband," she said, her voice barely above a whisper.

"That's not all," Mike said. "God, this is a fuck-up beyond all proportions. The commissioner has asked me to personally oversee this investigation." He took a sip of water. "After the charges against you were dropped," he said, indicating to Rupe, "the pressure increased on the local force to find out what happened. The media ran several campaigns, and when the lack of a viable suspect ramped up the pressure, I was asked to temporarily transfer a few of my senior officers over to Kennington to bolster the investigation. After some damned fine police work, we were able to bring Mr Reynolds in for questioning. He crumbled pretty quickly once we presented him with the facts."

"What was his motive?" Rupe asked.

Mike steepled his fingers under his chin. "It turns out that Mrs Reynolds told Mr Reynolds she was leaving him. For you."

Jayne swivelled her head in Rupe's direction so quickly she damn near broke her neck. "Is this true?"

Rupe remained as calm as ever, although Jayne did spot a slight tightening of the skin around his mouth at her challenge. "No, it's not true. Vanessa was a temporary distraction. Even if she'd been single, I wouldn't have wanted anything more permanent."

Jayne twisted back around in her seat, but the maelstrom of emotions swirling within her must have shown on her face, because he covered her hand with his and squeezed, an attempt at reassurance.

"Anyway," Mike continued, either oblivious to the emotional undercurrent between her and Rupe or deciding to ignore it, "Mr

Reynolds, whose influence stretches far and wide, used some contacts and pulled in a few favours. The reason why you can't remember very much from that night, Mr Fox-Whittingham, is because your drinks were spiked. You don't remember walking back to Mrs Reynolds's hotel room because you didn't. You were driven there by an assassin Mr Reynolds hired. Once you were both out of it, the hitman injected Mrs Reynolds with a massive overdose of heroin, one that she wouldn't have stood a chance of surviving."

"Jesus." Rupe ran a hand over the top of his head. "I still don't understand why, though. Even if he did think Nessa and I were running off into the sunset together, that's hardly a reason to kill her. From what Nessa told me, their marriage was a sham anyway."

"It seems that when Mrs Reynolds told her husband she was leaving him, he threatened to cut her off, to make sure she left penniless. He also said he'd throw Mrs Reynolds's mother, who has Alzheimer's, out of the nursing home that he was paying for. Mrs Reynolds decided to hit back. She told him that she knew all about his dodgy dealings over the years, and she threatened to expose him, to report them to the police and the newspapers." Mike shrugged. "So he had her killed and set you up as the fall guy."

Jayne frowned and shook her head slightly. "But how do Fisher and the drug pusher fit into all this?"

Mike closed his eyes briefly. "What I'm about to say stays within these four walls for now. Do I make myself clear?"

Rupe and Jayne nodded.

"That's what I meant before when I said we had a right fuck-up on our hands. Fisher and Sean Reynolds knew each other from way back. They grew up on the same estate, but their lives obviously took very different directions. Reynolds found out about Fisher's sister, and he used it as leverage to persuade Fisher to help him get you, Mr Fox-Whittingham, sent down for Mrs

Reynolds's murder—in exchange for a tidy sum, of course, which Fisher would receive if you were found guilty. Fisher jumped at the chance. Not only would he get revenge for his sister's death, but he'd also be able to quit the force, to live the kind of life that he always thought was owed to him."

Rupe's hand tightened around Jayne's as she shuffled even farther forwards in her seat. "So Fisher copped to all this?"

A faint flush crept up Mike's neck, and he shook his head. "We don't know where he is. Uniform went to pick him up yesterday, but he'd scarpered. His flat had been cleared of all personal items and his bank account emptied. We've put out an alert. He won't get far. In the meantime, Mr Fox-Whittingham, I suggest you remain vigilant until we have Fisher in custody. He clearly has a vendetta against you, and I can't say for sure that he won't act on that."

"Wow," Rupe said with a shake of his head. "I really appreciate you sharing this with me." He rubbed his fingertips over his lips. "Will I need to testify when it comes to trial?"

"Perhaps. That'll be up to the CPS. I'll keep you both updated." Mike grimaced. "And please keep this confidential. The media will get hold of this story soon enough, but I'd rather it was through an official statement, written by the police press office, than a leak that will cause fallout that we won't be able to control."

Jayne rose from her chair. "Thank you, Mike. And don't worry, this stays between us."

28

After Mike's jaw-dropping revelation, Rupe drove Jayne to her office with a promise to call by her apartment later that night. As she watched his car disappear down the road, a twinge of sadness that she wouldn't see him all day gnawed at her gut. She laughed at herself as she pushed open the door to her office building. She really did have it bad.

She rode the lift to her floor, and as the doors opened, her phone pinged with an incoming text. She dug it out of her bag, grinning when she saw the sender—and the message: *Wear the pink lingerie tonight.*

Desire pooled in the pit of her stomach. Damn, that man even had the Midas touch over SMS. Donna was on the phone as Jayne walked down the hallway towards her office. She swiped her calendar from Donna's outstretched hand and held up her other hand in greeting.

Once inside her office, she dumped her stuff on the desk and typed out a response: *It's being laundered.*

With a grin, she sat down and waited for his reply. She didn't have to wait long.

Then I'll bring some with me for you to model. Be ready. Be naked.

Her stomach flipped, and her excitement increased. She'd never sexted before, but God, there was something so thrilling and illicit about it.

Be hard, she wrote back, feeling like a naughty schoolgirl messing about at the back of the class.

I already am.

She was about to reply once more when a knock interrupted her. Irritated, she looked up as Donna poked her head around the door.

"You're not going to like this," she said with a grimace.

Jayne sighed. "What now?"

"Darren's called in sick. He mentioned something about projectile vomiting." Donna pulled a face. "And he was due in court this afternoon. Dangerous-driving case. That banking boss's son."

Jayne rubbed her eyes. "Which one is that again?"

"You remember, the young lad who drove his Ferrari down Kensington High Street at over sixty miles an hour and almost knocked that kid off his bike."

"Oh yeah, I remember now. I also remember Darren saying he was an arrogant little sod." She let out a resigned breath. "Can't anyone else fill in?"

Donna shook her head. "I'll email you the files. Darren said it should be straightforward but to give him a call if you have any questions."

Jayne groaned as Donna closed the door. She'd hoped for a quiet day and an early finish. Now she'd be lucky if she got home before nine. She sent a quick text to Rupe, telling him what had happened and that she'd call when she was home.

By the time she set off for court at two that afternoon, her mood had taken a downward spiral. If rich boy got on her last remaining nerve, he'd feel the sharp edge of her tongue. With any luck, he'd plead guilty, and she'd be home by six. Darren's notes had confirmed that the little shit hadn't cared to enlighten his lawyer about which way he was intending to plead. Honestly, sometimes she questioned whether she'd picked the right side. At times like these, the thought of being a prosecutor and being able to put lowlifes behind bars seemed rather appealing.

As luck would have it, Daddy persuaded son to do the decent thing—probably for the first time in his life—and he pleaded guilty. The son got a suspended sentence, community service, and a hefty fine, which wouldn't make much of a dent in Daddy's bonus for that year. After several profuse thank-yous from the father and a sullen "Thanks" from the son—even as he refused to look her in the eye—Jayne managed to get on the tube for six thirty. She considered sending Rupe a text telling him she was on her way home, but after rushing round all day in the heat, she was desperate for a shower. If she texted him, he'd probably get to her place before she did, and while he might not mind sweaty breasts and clammy thighs, she did.

She nudged open the door to her apartment and dropped the stack of files she was carrying. They landed on the floor with a hollow thud. Kicking off her shoes, she simultaneously tossed her jacket over the back of the couch and then padded into the bathroom. She shucked the rest of her clothes and dived under a cool shower. *God*, that felt good. After a few minutes enjoying the refreshing spray, she quickly dried her hair, already getting the wonderful fluttering in her belly at the thought of what Rupe would do to her when he came over.

She wandered back into the living room and picked up her phone, the sight sending her heart rate ramping up. A text from Rupe:

Jayne, I need you to come to my place. It's urgent. Please hurry.

With a frown, Jayne dialled his number. It rang out without him picking up, but weirdly, it didn't divert to his voicemail either. She tried again. Still no answer. With anxiety clawing at her gut, she quickly dressed and darted outside. After shifting from foot to foot, she eventually gave up on the lift and ran into the stairwell. She almost fell over her own feet as she scrambled downstairs, and by the time she got to the foyer of her apartment building, her lungs were burning from overexertion and the beginnings of mild panic. She reached into her pocket to try calling Rupe again. *Shit.* She'd left her phone in the apartment. *Sod it. No time to go back.* She needed to get over to Rupe's.

As she stepped into the street, something hard prodded at her side, and a firm hand gripped her around her waist.

"That's a gun jammed in your ribs," a vaguely familiar voice hissed in her ear. "Don't do anything stupid, Jayne."

She froze as the discomfort in her side increased.

"Unless you want to be responsible for the death of several innocent people, not to mention your own, you will do exactly as I say."

Jayne searched the deep recesses of her terrified mind, eventually coming up with the answer.

"Detective Fisher," she whispered.

"Not just a pretty face, are you, Jayne? Now, move!"

He prodded her with the butt of the gun, propelling her towards a large dark-blue estate car parked on double yellow lines outside her apartment building. Jayne's gaze darted around as she tried to assess her chances of shouting for help, but his warning about harming innocents made her clamp her mouth shut.

Fisher opened the passenger door and shoved her inside. He immediately crowded her, his chest pressing against hers as he picked up two sets of handcuffs from the driver's seat. Jayne recoiled at the smell of stale sweat and anxiety that came off him in waves. She tried to get her knee up, but the angle was all wrong. As she wriggled, Fisher slammed his fist into her stomach. Jayne's breath left her body in a rush, and she grunted. Fisher snapped the handcuffs around her wrists and yanked her arms overhead, securing the other end to the bars of the head restraint.

As he ran around the front of the car, Jayne tried to catch her breath. She stared hopefully out of the window, but the tinting was far too dark for anyone to see a woman in distress. Fisher threw himself in the driver's seat. He rammed the car into first gear and sped away.

"Fisher, what are you doing?" she said, trying to keep her voice steady and even, despite the panic growing like a rampant weed inside her. She tried not to think about the text from Rupe and what it might mean. What if Fisher had hurt him, or worse?

Fisher shot her a look before turning his attention back to the road. Sweat poured from his brow, and he had several days' beard growth, which, along with his rumpled clothing, gave him a desperate, almost unhinged air.

"Look, if you cut me loose now, there's no harm done."

Fisher continued to ignore her, and Jayne scrabbled around in her brain, trying to remember his first name. Perhaps if she engaged with him on a more personal level, she had a chance of him listening to her. What had Frank said when she and Rupe had met him in the pub? *Come on, Jayne. Think!* The answer came to her in a rush.

"Think of your family, John. Your parents," she said in a placating tone. The use of his first name caused Fisher to set his eyes on her once more, his gaze darting between her and the road ahead.

"Fuck my parents," he growled. "If they hadn't been such losers, I'd have had a chance of a better life."

"Then think of your career. This is still salvageable." *Unless you've hurt Rupe, and then I'll make you suffer, you complete psycho.*

Fisher expelled a harsh laugh. "Don't treat me like an idiot. Of course it's not salvageable. *They know everything!* They've arrested Sean, and he's singing like a fucking canary. Now shut the fuck up unless you want a smack in the mouth."

His breathing grew harsh as he pressed down the accelerator. The car sped up. They were heading out of London, tracking east.

Jayne tried to keep an eye on her surroundings, but darkness had descended, making the task almost impossible. She estimated that they'd been driving for about an hour when Fisher stopped the car. He jumped out and opened a gate before driving into a field. After closing the gate, he drove to the far side of the field before yanking the steering wheel to the left. He maneuvered the car up a narrow dirt path. The shrubs on either side scraped against the bodywork of the vehicle, scattering twigs and leaves to the ground. After five minutes, the track opened out onto a small clearing. Ahead stood a single-story building—disused and neglected, with missing roof tiles and boarded-up windows. Cold fingers of dread inched up Jayne's spine as Fisher parked the car around the back of the property.

He cut the engine and climbed out. He wrenched open Jayne's door, unlocked the handcuffs, and hauled her outside. With a hard shove, he slammed her face-first against the bonnet of the car. A searing pain burst through her cheekbone, and she screamed. Fisher jerked her arms behind her and locked the handcuffs around both her wrists.

He leaned farther over her, his foul-smelling breath making her gag. "Not so fucking sure of yourself now are you, Miss Stuck-Up Lawyer?" he hissed in her ear. "Don't think I didn't notice the way you looked down your nose at me."

"John, please let me go," she said, her voice tinged with panic.

Fisher grabbed her by the hair and hauled her to her feet. Jayne cried out as her scalp burned.

"Scream as much as you like." He roughly shoved her in the direction of the ramshackle building. "No one will hear you out here."

29

Rupe frowned at the clock and then glanced down at the text Jayne had sent earlier in the day. Almost ten hours had passed, and still no word from her. Surely she couldn't still be at work? He called up the opening hours of the courthouse. Nine to five. That meant it had been closed for four hours.

He dialled Jayne's number, but it rang out without connecting. He stabbed out a quick text to her, grabbed his jacket and keys, and headed over to her apartment.

Rupe abandoned his car in a no-parking zone and ran inside the building. He called Jayne again on the way upstairs, but there was still no answer. Something felt wrong. He didn't know what, but in the time he'd known her, Jayne was never without her phone, and even if she couldn't answer, she'd always sent a short text.

As he reached the door to her apartment, he banged hard.

"Jayne, are you in there? Open up."

Silence.

He banged again, and when there was still no answer, he called her. A faint ringing tone sounded from inside the apartment, and Rupe's heart shot into overdrive. If her phone was inside, where the fuck was she? What if she'd hurt herself and was lying unconscious inside?

When his furious knocking went unanswered, Rupe tore off downstairs to the building superintendent's office. He pushed open the door. The super was watching a boxing match on the TV and glanced over his shoulder with an irritated expression at the interruption.

"Heard of knocking, buddy?" he said.

"I need you to open up Jayne Seymour's apartment. Number 1146."

"Sorry, pal," the guy said, leaning back in his chair, his hands laced over his enormous stomach. "No can do. Building rules."

Rupe slammed his palms on the messy desk and leaned forward. His eyes fell on the nametag pinned to the guy's shirt. "I couldn't give a *shit* about the rules, Dwayne. She's not answering the door, and yet I can hear her phone ringing inside."

Dwayne pushed back his chair to put a bit of distance between himself and an increasingly angry Rupe. "Well, maybe she don't want to be disturbed." He grinned then. "You kids have a fight?"

Rupe's arm shot out, and he fisted Dwayne's shirt. Despite the weight difference, Rupe effortlessly yanked him out of his chair.

Dwayne's eyes bulged. "Hey, that's assault."

Rupe got right up in his face. "I don't give a flying fuck. Now, either you open Jayne Seymour's door with a key, or I am going to put your head through it. Your choice."

Dwayne's hands shot in the air. "Okay, buddy. Take it easy."

Rupe let go. Dwayne stumbled a little before regaining his balance. He opened a cupboard fixed to the wall. Inside were row upon row of keys. "Apartment 1146, you said?"

"Yes."

Dwayne's chubby finger trailed across the individual keys,

making Rupe's impatience levels soar. Eventually, the building superintendent found what he was looking for and unhooked it.

They took the lift up to Jayne's floor because there was no way Dwayne would make eleven flights of stairs without having an asthma attack or collapsing from exhaustion. As Dwayne fumbled with getting the key in the lock, Rupe dialled Jayne once more. The ringing tone got louder as the door opened. Rupe shoved past Dwayne into the apartment.

"Jayne," he called out as he crossed the open-plan living space and opened her bedroom door. The bed was made, her dressing gown in a heap on the floor. Rupe went into the bathroom. Damp towels. So she'd taken a very recent shower, but there was absolutely no sign of her.

He walked back into the living room and picked up her phone, cursing when he realised it was password protected. He downloaded a software programme he'd written to his own phone and ran the script. Within a minute, he'd unlocked the security on Jayne's phone and broken the law at the same time. Too bad. He'd apologise later.

He went into her recent calls list. She'd made several during the day. A couple to her partner, one to her PA, and a few with names he didn't recognise, which he guessed were clients. And two to him about an hour ago—that he hadn't received.

With a growing sense of unease, he glanced over at Dwayne, who was hovering by the door.

"You can go," Rupe said dismissively.

"I can't leave you in here, buddy. I'll lose my job."

"Fuck's sake," Rupe muttered. Still, it didn't matter any more. Jayne wasn't there, but at least he had her phone. "Fine. I'm leaving."

He stepped into the hallway and waited around long enough to make sure Dwayne locked up, then he tore downstairs. He'd lucked out, because his car hadn't been towed or even ticketed.

He drove to a legal spot and pulled up the list of numbers Jayne had called.

He contacted every one. None of them had seen Jayne. He'd tried not to worry Darren, but he could hear the concerned tone in Jayne's partner's voice.

Next, he opened her text programme—and his heart nearly stopped when he saw the text she'd received under his name. With escalating alarm, he went back to Jayne's contacts and found the number he needed.

∼

By the time he arrived at the home of Detective Chief Superintendent Mike Wilson, Rupe was in full-on panic mode. Mike opened the door with a baby slung over his shoulder, his large hand rubbing in circles over the screaming kid's back.

"Sorry, my wife is at her sister's, so it's my turn to babysit," he said with a roll of his eyes as he ushered Rupe inside.

"I'm really sorry to bother you," Rupe said as Mike finished winding the baby and put her down in her cot, where she quit crying and decided to gurgle instead.

"It's not a bother. You were a bit garbled on the phone. Clue me in."

Rupe took a breath. "I can't find Jayne. She's not at home, no one at work has seen her since she left for court this afternoon, and yet there were signs that she'd been at her apartment very recently, not to mention that she'd left her phone behind."

Mike frowned as he rubbed his mouth. "That's strange. No sign of a struggle?"

Rupe shook his head. "The weirdest thing is this." He pulled up the text and passed the phone to Mike. "I didn't send that."

Mike tilted his head to one side. "But it's come up as you. Now, I'm no technological genius, but doesn't that mean the number it was sent from coincides with the number against the contact in Jayne's phone?"

"Ordinarily, yes, but it's not impossible to fake."

Mike ran a hand over the top of his head. "Okay, I'll call it in. Normally, I'd wait at least until tomorrow, but as this is so out of character for Jayne, I'll get the guys on it now."

"Thank you," Rupe said.

Within half an hour, a couple of detectives arrived at Mike's house, and the four of them sat around Mike's dining room table as Rupe shared what little he knew. He kept having to wipe clammy hands on his pants as his panic and worry increased with every second that Jayne was missing.

"Who would take her?" Rupe asked when the detectives put their notebooks away.

"We don't know that anyone's taken her," Mike said. "Let's not jump to conclusions until we know more."

"Of course someone's taken her," Rupe said, his voice escalating along with his fear.

And then an idea hit him. "What if it's Fisher?"

Mike's eyebrows shot up. "I'll accept that Fisher is in a lot of trouble. He's a desperate man, but desperate enough to turn to kidnap? I'm not sure." He patted Rupe on the shoulder. "I know it's difficult, but try not to worry. I'm sure Jayne going missing is something completely innocent."

Rupe briefly closed his eyes and prayed Mike was right.

30

Jayne tried to bend her arms, but due to the angle that Fisher had handcuffed her to the chair, she couldn't. Her arms began to cramp, and she fidgeted as shooting pains shot through her biceps and up to her shoulders.

Her mouth was dry, her lips cracked, and she began to fantasise about Rupe crashing through the rickety old door and saving her. That meant she had to be hallucinating, because she was an independent woman who was perfectly capable of saving herself —as soon as she worked out how to impersonate Houdini.

Panic began to rush through her body, making her limbs tremble and any remaining saliva in her mouth disappear. What did Fisher want? After dumping her there and making sure she had no chance of escape, he'd disappeared. That had been hours ago, although she had no idea exactly how much time had passed.

God. I could die in this place.

Another shooting pain darted up her arm, and she sat as tall as the handcuffs allowed, which gave her a tinge of relief.

The door rattled, and daylight flooded the shack momentarily before Fisher slammed the door behind him. He came inside with a Tesco carrier bag. The normality of him walking in with a bag from a supermarket clashed with the terror of her situation. She glared at him with barely contained hatred, which probably wasn't too smart, but she was beyond caring. After years of unhappiness with Kyle, she'd finally moved on with Rupe and had stitched together her shattered self-esteem and self-worth. She would *not* allow this bastard to wreck all her hard work.

"Thirsty, Jayne?" he said, waving a plastic bottle of water in her face. Despite an intense yearning to feel the cool liquid soothing her ravaged throat, she shrugged nonchalantly. Fisher laughed, the sound hollow and more than a little scary. He appeared unhinged, his hair even more unkempt than usual, his eyes wild as he paced up and down. Once again, fear rushed through her system, making it difficult to think straight. She couldn't allow anxiety to cloud her vision. She needed to keep a clear head and wait for her opportunity—if one ever came.

Fisher unscrewed the bottle and thrust it between her lips. With a painful grip on her hair, he tipped her head back. Water rushed into her mouth, and she struggled to swallow. The cool liquid eased her thirst. *God, it feels good.*

Before she'd had her fill, he tore the bottle away from her lips. Her eyes greedily followed his hands as he screwed the top back on the bottle. He dug around in the plastic bag and pulled out a pack of sandwiches.

"Hope you don't mind tuna," he said, whipping the cellophane wrapping from around the cardboard and pulling out a limp sandwich that had definitely seen better days.

Jayne *hated* tuna, but right then, she'd eat anything. She had to keep her strength up, and turning down the only food Fisher was likely to share wouldn't be the smartest move.

He tore off a piece of sandwich. Jayne opened her mouth, and his little finger touched her bottom lip as he slipped the bread inside. She almost baulked but then managed to chew and swallow.

"There's a good girl," he said.

The condescending prick. The minute she got her chance, he'd be wearing his balls as earrings. He gave her another couple of pieces of sandwich, until she firmly clamped her lips together and jerked her head back.

"Your loss," he said with a shrug. He wolfed down the rest of the sandwich, along with a pork pie. The sound of his chewing, all slop and no manners, made her grind her teeth. Once he'd finished, he dusted off his hands and shoved the empty packets inside the plastic bag. He tossed it in the corner, and when he turned back around, he had a dirty rag in his hands. Jayne's eyes widened as he stalked towards her.

"You don't need to gag me," she said. "Please don't."

Fisher ignored her. He rammed the balled-up gag in her mouth and secured it with grey duct tape. Jayne forced herself to stay calm, to keep breathing steadily through her nose. The rag tasted of oil and grease. *Oh God.* She couldn't vomit, not with this in her mouth. She'd choke.

Fisher stood back and examined his handiwork. He gave a satisfied nod followed by an equally satisfied smile. "That should do it."

Do what?

He reached into his pocket and pulled out a compact camera. He pointed it at her face, and when the flash went off, it almost blinded her. She flinched and blinked, and squeezed her eyes shut. Fisher slapped her hard, and her eyes flew open, her cheek throbbing from his assault—the same cheek he'd slammed into the car bonnet. She could feel the swelling spreading towards her eye socket. He took a couple more pictures.

"Okay, Jayne, here's how this is going to go down. Your rich-as-fuck boyfriend killed the only person who was there for me, who understood me, who loved me for who I *am*, not who everyone thought I should be. My plan to see him rot in prison backfired somewhat, so I had to make a new plan."

His chest heaved as his anger rolled through him. Jayne could sense the fury building, and fear for her safety soared.

"Now, the lower classes of this country know all too well that money talks. And Rupert Fox-Whittingham has more than his fair share. More than he *deserves*. So I'm going to do him a favour. In return for sending you back in one piece..." Fisher paused as a slow, maddened smile crept across his face. "*Almost* in one piece, he's going to transfer a large amount of cash to a bank account of my choosing—and he's going to make sure I get out of the country to one without an extradition order. I'm thinking Rio would suit me."

Jayne shook her head. The guy was crazy. Rupe didn't have the sort of power to guarantee safe passage. The police wouldn't agree to a deal like that for the return of someone like her. She was a nobody, at least to them. To Rupe, she was somebody, even though the longer she was away from him, the more her certainty in Rupe's feelings faded, until their connection almost seemed like a dream.

Fisher ripped off the duct tape, taking several strands of hair from Jayne's already tender head. He yanked the gag from her mouth and threw it to one side. Relief swept through her. At least he wasn't going to leave her with the foul-tasting rag in her mouth. Without saying another word, he gathered up the plastic bag, dropped the camera back in his pocket, and went outside, securely padlocking the door behind him.

Her head lolled forwards as exhaustion and terror swept through her body, but then she took a deep breath and gave herself a talking-to. At some point, her chance would come. And when it did, she'd be ready.

31

"Okay, I'm officially in the doghouse, but my wife is on her way home." Mike tossed his phone on the table and tried—yet failed—to comfort his screaming daughter.

"I'm sorry," Rupe said, having to raise his voice to compete with the bawling kid. "But I didn't want this being treated as a normal missing-person case, which it would have been if I'd simply called it in."

Mike gave a wry smile. "Don't worry about it. To be honest, I'm regularly in the doghouse, so nothing new there."

Rupe's lips twitched briefly before despair swamped him once more. He glanced at his watch. Four in the morning. "Where is she?" he muttered.

Before Mike could answer, Rupe's phone pinged. *Unknown number.* He swiped the screen, and all the blood drained from his face.

"Oh, God," he said, his voice harsh and rasping. He turned the phone to face Mike.

"Shit." Mike snatched the phone from Rupe's trembling hand.

His brows were pulled low as he examined the photograph of Jayne. *His* Jayne. Bound and gagged, battered and bruised.

Anger rolled through him. Whoever had Jayne would pay. Whatever it took.

His phone pinged with another text, and before Mike could react, Rupe had snatched his phone back and read:

Fifty million pounds and transport to a nonextradition country of my choice, or she dies. You have three days.

"Now we know it's Fisher." Rupe turned the screen around so Mike could read the message.

Mike frowned. "It doesn't say that."

Rupe launched himself to his feet and began to pace, his mind working overtime as he pieced it all together. "Think about it. Fisher wants revenge for my supposed culpability in his sister's death. He agrees to help Sean Reynolds fit me up, but that falls apart, and then Reynolds blabs. Fisher is furious—all his carefully laid plans turning to shit. He needs a way out, fast. He wants me to suffer, so he snatches Jayne."

Mike rubbed his chin. "That makes sense, but we can't ignore the possibility it isn't him."

"So what do we do now?"

"Send the text and the photo to my phone, and I'll call it in."

Rupe tossed his hands in the air. "That's it? Shouldn't I start to get the money together or something?"

"No. Hang fire."

Mike grabbed his phone and disappeared outside. Rupe did as Mike asked, then he sank into the nearest chair and covered his face with his hands. He shouldn't have let Jayne out of his sight. As soon as they'd found out about Fisher, he should have realised the danger. Mike had warned him to stay vigilant, but neither he nor the detective had even thought about danger to Jayne. He fisted clumps of his hair. *Why didn't I see this coming?* Whatever Mike said, Rupe knew the only logical answer was that Fisher had her.

He hated doing nothing, despised sitting on his hands while Fisher held all the cards. And then it came to him—the new tracking software he and Aaron had been working on. He shouted through to Mike that he'd call him later and jumped into his car.

By the time he reached Aaron's apartment building in Canary Wharf, the morning rush hour had begun, and he had to dodge commuters streaming off buses and trains as they headed into the financial capital for another normal day. Except that day was anything but normal for Rupe. No doubt it would bring angst and worry and terror as Fisher moved the chess pieces.

Aaron took an age to come to the door, despite Rupe's furious banging. Chains rattled and door locks eased into their housings before Aaron opened up, bleary-eyed and confused.

"Rupe, it's my bloody day off. What the hell are you doing here?"

"I know." Rupe eased past, catching sight of a half-naked redhead sprawled on Aaron's bed.

With an apologetic grin, Aaron closed the bedroom door.

"Sorry to disturb," Rupe said, urgency leaking into his voice. "But I need your help."

Aaron's momentary embarrassment at being caught with a woman who wasn't his girlfriend disappeared as he latched on to Rupe's tone. "Of course, anything. Here, have a seat."

Rupe collapsed into the offered chair and ran a hand roughly over the top of his head. "You know that tracking software we've been working on?"

Aaron nodded. "Yeah."

"What's the latest beta test look like?"

"Over ninety-five per cent accuracy."

Rupe's eyebrows shot up. "That good?"

Aaron nodded. "Another couple of weeks, and we'll hit close to one hundred. What's this about?"

Rupe briefly apprised him of the situation with Jayne before handing over his phone. "There's a picture and a text. No number. I need you to run this through the latest version, trace what phone it came from, and then give me the location details."

Aaron's eyes lit up. He was a pure techie at heart, but as CEO of one of Rupe's most successful companies, he didn't get to fiddle about much these days. The tracking-software project had given him a welcome diversion from strategy decisions, balance sheets, and cash-flow statements.

Aaron briefly checked out the texts Fisher had sent. "We'll need to go into the office."

Rupe stood and took back his phone. "Get dressed."

Aaron disappeared into the bedroom. His quiet but firm voice drifted into the living room, followed by a much louder, higher-pitched one. He had to be telling his latest conquest to ship out. Sure enough, two minutes later, Aaron and the woman appeared. She gave Rupe a scathing look before slinging her bag over her shoulder and slamming the door on her way out.

Rupe raised an eyebrow. "Feisty."

Aaron chuckled. "She'll get over it."

They took Rupe's car to the office. Aaron booted up his computer and pulled a chair around so he and Rupe could both see the screen.

Once the operating system had gone through its checks, Aaron started up the test software. He inserted a USB cable into his laptop and held out his hand. "Give me your phone again."

Aaron plugged the other end of the USB cord into the computer and clicked through a few screens, feeding the software a few pertinent facts. After a couple of seconds, a bar appeared with the word "Searching" beneath it. As Rupe watched the bar edge to the right, the percentage completion increasing, a growing sense of impatience made his foot tap and his fingers drum on the desk.

After five minutes, when the damn server hadn't returned any results, Rupe got to his feet and stared down at the street.

Hundreds of people darted about far below him, going about their business, while his life was on hold. He glanced over his shoulder.

"Is that normal?" he said, pointing his chin at the circle whirring around on Aaron's screen.

"Yes. I've been trying to speed it up but haven't had much success yet."

"As soon as I've got Jayne back, I'll make it my number-one priority," Rupe said, the focus on work staving off the terrible churning in his gut. Every second wasted was a second more that Jayne was in danger.

Aaron reached into his desk drawer and pulled out a bottle of whiskey and two glasses. "Here. And don't give me any grief about drinking this early. It's still my day off, and you look like you need it."

"I wasn't about to give you grief." Rupe took the glass from Aaron and threw back the whiskey, the burn welcome and distracting. He bent down and peered at the screen. "Almost there."

"Yes, should return a result in a couple of minutes. I hope it finds something."

Rupe grimaced. "Not as much as I do." At that moment, the screen changed, and a mobile number appeared.

"Yes!" hissed Rupe. "Now trace it."

"It'll only work if the phone is switched on."

"I know."

Aaron opened another programme and entered the phone number into it. The app returned immediate results.

Not found

Rupe slammed his hands on the desk. "Goddammit."

Aaron clapped him on the back. "The good news is we have the number, and he'll have to switch his phone on at some point because he'll need to make contact. I'll set up a constant sweep, and as soon as it finds something, I'll transfer the details straight to your phone."

"Thanks, man," Rupe said. "Want a lift home?"

"Nah. You've ruined my first day off in a month. Might as well stay here now."

Rupe half smiled. Aaron was a workaholic. It was one of the reasons Rupe had hired him to run the London operation. Well, that and the fact that the man was a technological genius. Sometimes he made Rupe look like a slouch, but then Rupe would use that as a kick up the arse to improve his own skills.

"Thanks again. I'll call you." Rupe climbed in to his car and rested his forehead against the steering wheel. Anxiety swarmed in his gut, giving him a fluttery, hollow feeling. He started the engine and headed for home.

As he pulled up outside his house, his phone pinged with an incoming text. His heart leaped into his throat. It was from Mike:

I'm at the station. Incident team up and running. Don't come down. You'll only get in the way. I'll call you later.

A modicum of comfort swept through him. Thank God Mike had the clout and resources at his fingertips to move this quickly. Rupe considered tapping out a quick text telling Mike about the breakthrough with the tracking software, but he decided to wait and see if Aaron could locate Fisher first. No point waving a red flag on illegal activity if he didn't need to.

He trudged into the house, his eyes stinging from lack of sleep, his chest prickling with stress and worry. He steeled himself for Abi's well-intentioned but overprotective mothering, but the house was quiet. As he entered the kitchen, he spotted a note she'd stuck to the fridge door: "Out shopping. Back later."

He rolled his eyes. No matter how many times he told Abi to order in from Ocado, she preferred the old-fashioned act of trawling around a supermarket.

He touched the coffee pot. Still hot. After pouring a cup, he wandered into the living room and collapsed into a chair. Was it only yesterday that he and Jayne had been called to Mike's office and told about Fisher? God, it seemed like much longer than that.

After hours with no word from Mike or Aaron, Rupe began to lose hope. Didn't they say the first twenty-four hours were critical, or was that for murder inquiries? From what Rupe knew about Fisher, he didn't fear for Jayne's life—at least not yet. As long as Fisher thought he had a chance of pulling this off—escaping capture and grabbing the cash—Jayne's life wouldn't be in danger. No, what worried Rupe much more was what Fisher was doing to her in the meantime. He'd already proved he wouldn't hesitate to hit a woman. What else was he capable of?

The room grew dim. Rupe glanced at the clock on his laptop. *Eight fifteen.* Jayne had been missing for over twenty-four hours. His heart cramped as he thought of her alone, scared, and in pain. What if she was hungry or thirsty? Oh God, he felt *useless*. He stepped over to the decanter of whiskey in the corner of his office, but before he could take out the stopper, his phone dinged.

Rupe snatched it off his desk and saw a text from Aaron: *He's on.*

His pulse jolted, and his heart sped up. With shaking hands, he opened the app. Within seconds, a map appeared, and then a red dot. The dot was moving, signalling that the owner of the phone was on the move, and at that speed, he was using some sort of transport.

Rupe ran downstairs and threw himself into his car. He floored the accelerator and set off for the police station. Fisher was on borrowed time.

32

Jayne jerked awake, her back screaming in agony, the muscles in her shoulders spasming, and her bladder fit to burst. She peered into the darkness, and after a couple of minutes, shapes began to form. How long had it been since Fisher had left? With the windows boarded up, she had no sense of time.

She tried to shift a little in the chair. Every part of her was numb. The only saving grace was that it was summer. If she'd been taken in winter, the cold would have made her situation even more grim.

She clenched her pelvic floor, which gave a momentary reprieve from the desperate need to pee, but the minute she released her inner muscles, the pain roared back. She had no choice. She was going to have to let it go. She relaxed her bladder. Rather than embarrassment, she felt a strong sense of relief.

Something rustled in the corner. Jayne strained her eyes, recoiling when her gaze fell on an enormous rat. *Oh hell.* She wasn't exactly afraid of the large rodents, but she didn't fancy having to fight the bugger off, particularly with her limited range of movement. As long as it stayed on its side of the ramshackle hut, she wouldn't freak out.

The sound of a car engine reached her, slowly getting closer and closer. She heard a door slam, feet running. The door to the shack was flung open. A torch shone in her eyes. She flinched and turned her head to the side.

"Urgh, you dirty bitch," Fisher spat out. "You fucking reek."

Jayne set her jaw, and despite being at a serious disadvantage and worried about what he might do, she let rip. "Well, what the hell did you expect me to do, you bloody idiot? No toilet, no ability to go even if there had been one because you've got me tied to this fucking chair! And you've been gone for hours!"

Fisher stuck the torch in his mouth and unlocked her handcuffs. Jayne shook out her hands as blood flowed to her extremities, the agony almost unbearable.

He yanked her to her feet. "Well, lucky for you, I've found better accommodation." His hand tightened around her upper arm, and he shoved her towards the door. She stumbled before righting herself. As he propelled her outside, his grip loosened slightly. Jayne took a deep breath and slammed her elbow backwards, towards his ribs. Fisher grunted and released her. Jayne took off. She ignored the pain in the soles of her bare feet and her burning lungs as she stumbled into the night.

She had no idea where she was going. All she could see was blackness. She stuck her hands out in front and carried on running. Damn, but the countryside was dark and more than a little scary. She wanted to turn around, to check whether Fisher was behind her, but she was too scared. She had to keep going and hope she was heading towards civilisation.

Her foot caught a tree root and she sprawled to the ground. She cried out as her ankle twisted beneath her.

"There you are, you fucking bitch." Fisher grabbed her hair and hauled her to her feet. Jayne screamed in agony as yet another chunk of her hair came away from her scalp. She stumbled as Fisher dragged her back to the car. He threw her onto the rear seats and climbed on top of her, his knees digging painfully into her thighs. Jayne struggled and swung her fists, but Fisher was too quick. He captured her wrists in one of his hands. His other fist came towards her face. Jayne tried to turn away, but his punch connected, and her cheek exploded in agony.

With her head swimming, she struggled to focus. Fisher yanked one of her arms straight, and she felt the scratch of a needle. Her eyes grew too heavy to keep open. Her last thought was *I'm fucked.*

∾

RUPE ABANDONED his car in the only available space—a disabled one—when he arrived at the station. He pushed open the door, and it bounced off the hinges. A middle-aged couple seated on grey plastic chairs briefly looked up before the woman resumed her rocking and murmuring under her breath. The man absent-mindedly patted her hand.

"I need to see Mike Wilson. Now," Rupe said to the copper behind the front desk.

"Is that right." The sergeant in charge looked up from his crossword with an arched eyebrow. "Do you have an appointment?"

"No."

"Then take a seat, sir," he said, pointing at the row of chairs. "I'll have to see if I can get hold of him. What's it about?"

"Fuck this," Rupe muttered, shaking his head. He ignored the sergeant's question and dialled Mike's number. After what seemed like an age, Mike answered.

"I'm downstairs," Rupe said. "Your desk sergeant is being a little obstructive."

Mike chuckled. "That's what we pay them for. Hang on, I'm coming down."

Rupe gave the sergeant a triumphant look, but the man simply shrugged and returned to completing the crossword. About five minutes later, Mike appeared and indicated for Rupe to follow him down a hallway that was in desperate need of a lick of paint.

"How are you doing?" Mike said as they entered his office. He invited Rupe to sit down.

"I have a lock on Fisher."

Mike's eyes widened. "How?"

Rupe called up the app on his phone. The red dot was stationary, its blinking like a huge beacon calling out. "That's him."

A flush spread across Mike's neck. "Can you zoom in?"

Rupe nodded. He double-clicked on the screen until the app had drilled down to show road names.

"How did you get this?" Mike said, disbelief mingling with excitement in his voice.

"You don't want to know," Rupe said with a grimace.

Mike shook his head. "In that case, you're right. I don't."

Rupe gave a faint smile, but it fell when a text appeared. Fisher. Rupe and Mike took a sharp intake of breath. With his heart pounding in his chest, Rupe opened the message. Another picture of Jayne, this time Fisher had her splayed out in the back seat of a car. Her eyes were closed, and her cheek appeared even more swollen. Underneath, Fisher had written two words: *Tick Tock.*

Rupe lurched to his feet. "Let's go get him."

"Hang on. We need to do this the right way. I'll brief the team."

Rupe scowled. "One of *your* officers is holding *my* girlfriend. If you won't do anything, I will."

Mike rose from his chair and placed his hands flat on his desk. "If you go barrelling in, all guns blazing, we don't know what he'll do. Let me handle this, please. I know what I'm doing, and in case it has slipped your notice, I've known Jayne a lot longer than you. I am equally interested in bringing her home safe and sound as quickly as possible."

Rupe fixed Mike with a stare, and then his shoulders slumped. "Please just get her back."

Mike came around his desk and patted Rupe's shoulder. "We will."

At that moment, the red dot disappeared, and Rupe cursed.

"What does that mean?" Mike asked.

"He's switched off his phone. The app only works when it can get a bead on a signal." Rupe slammed his fist on Mike's desk. "Dammit. I bet that means he's on the move."

"But he'll have to switch it on again to contact us, so don't get too disheartened. We know where he is right now, and with any luck, that's also where he's keeping Jayne. I'll grab a couple of officers, and we'll check out that location. Even if she's not there, this is still more intel than we had five minutes ago. You can stay here in my office if you like."

Rupe shot Mike an incredulous look. "You actually think I'm going to stay here when Jayne is out there, hurt and scared?"

"That's exactly what I think. We could be going to a potential crime scene. I can't have civilians tramping about."

Rupe's lips clamped into a firm line. "Either I ride along with you, or I go alone. Your choice. The latter means I get there before you."

The two men stared at each other, one determined, the other reluctant. Eventually, Mike expelled a resigned sigh. "Fine. But you do exactly what I tell you. Got it?"

Rupe waited outside the incident room while Mike briefed his detectives. A couple of minutes later, he appeared with two suits and introduced them. The detectives—Barry and Steve—shook Rupe's hand, and the four of them headed out.

Rupe rode in the front of the car, which was unmarked, thank God—they didn't need to signal their arrival—while Barry and

Steve climbed in the back. Mike tapped some details into a sat nav system, and the mechanical voice gave them directions.

About an hour later, the sat nav announced that they'd arrived at their destination. They were surrounded by countryside and very little else. Rupe and Mike shared a look.

"This can't be it," Rupe said. "There's nothing here."

"Let's get out and look around." Mike cut the engine, and the four of them began walking up and down the road. Rupe wandered away from the others as his initial hopes plummeted. They'd been sent on a wild goose chase. His app didn't work. He cursed and fisted his hands in his hair and tugged hard, the resulting pain a short-term distraction from his failure.

"Hey," Barry shouted, his muffled voice carried away on the wind. "Over here."

Rupe ran towards him. When he reached the detective, his pulse jumped. Set back a little way from the road was a padlocked five-bar gate leading into a field. Beyond that, a grassy path had turned into more of a dirt track. Recent tyre tracks meant a car had been there. *Could be a farmer, or it could be Fisher.*

"Get that padlock off," Mike ordered.

Steve jogged back to the car and returned with a set of bolt cutters. Within seconds, the padlock fell to the ground. He pushed the gate open. Mike fetched the car and drove through. As they all jumped back inside, Mike nudged Rupe's arm.

"Remember, you're here as an observer. No heroics."

Rupe nodded, even though he inwardly acknowledged that if they found Jayne or Fisher, Mike's instructions would be summarily ignored.

They drove to the far side of the field, where a narrow track appeared to their left.

"Down there," Rupe said.

Mike turned in, and after a short while, the track widened. All four of them spotted the hut at the same time.

"Stop," Rupe shouted. He threw himself outside while the car was still coming to a halt.

"Goddammit," Mike cursed behind him, but Rupe was beyond caring about protocol or procedures or the fact that Mike could end up in deep shit if something went wrong.

The door of the hut was locked, but the wood was so rotten that a couple of kicks to the middle sorted it. As the door flew open, the stench almost made Rupe retch. Rats scattered as they realised their haven had been breached. Animal faeces, urine, and mould all combined to assault his senses, but worse than all those things, Jayne wasn't there.

Mike shone a torch around the shack. The place had no fixtures or fittings or even furniture, except for a wooden straight-backed chair off to one side. Debris was scattered all over the floor.

The detectives began combing the floor. Then, as Mike's torch swept past the chair, Rupe saw it—a tiny silver hoop earring.

"Stop," Rupe said. "Go back."

Mike shone the torch to where Rupe was pointing.

Rupe bent down and picked it up. "This is Jayne's."

"You're right," Mike said, moving in for a closer look.

"So she *was* here." Rupe scrubbed his face with a weary hand. "And we're too late."

"Any more from that app of yours?"

Rupe took his phone out of his pocket and glanced at the screen. "No." Despair swamped him, and his shoulders sagged.

Mike turned to Steve. "Call this in. I want forensics all over this place and the surrounding area."

"Yes, sir," Steve replied.

Mike clapped Rupe on the back. "This is good news. We're getting closer."

Yeah, but will it be enough to save Jayne?

33

Jayne groaned as she regained consciousness. She struggled into a seated position. Searing pain throbbed in her right cheek, and she could only open her left eye. To make matters worse, whatever she'd been drugged with was playing havoc with her ability to think straight. Her brain felt as if someone had stuffed it with cotton wool, and her one good eye wouldn't focus properly.

She turned her head slowly and looked around. She was being kept in some sort of basement. The walls were damp and covered with green mould, the concrete floor was cold as ice, and a single bulb hung from a loose wire in the centre of the room, throwing off a dim glow.

She'd been restrained once again, her hands secured behind her back with cable ties this time, although fortunately her feet had been left free. She soon discovered that tugging against her restraints made the ties bite even more painfully into her skin and got her no further towards being free.

Jayne struggled to her feet and paced out her prison. It measured about twenty feet by fifteen, give or take. On the ceiling, off-centre, was a trap door with a rusty handle she'd have had no chance of reaching even if her hands weren't restrained—and no doubt it would be locked from the outside anyway.

Her breathing escalated rapidly, her heart thundering in her chest. Desperate to stop a full-on panic attack, she forced herself to breathe slowly in through her nose and out through her mouth. She had to calm down and think her way out of this situation. She was smart, fit, young… and scared shitless.

A cold sweat broke out on her face, and her stomach contracted hard. She heaved several times, although all that came up was a tiny amount of yellow bile, which she spat onto the floor. Her stomach felt bruised after its failed efforts, and she sank to the ground, her knees tight against her chest, but that position made her shoulders scream with pain, so she stood up again. She was *not* going to cry. No way was she going to give that bastard the satisfaction.

What if he just left her there to die? No food or water—days and days of suffering before her body finally gave out. She shook her head to dispel such morbid thoughts. Her one good eye was focusing better now that it had adjusted to the dim light. The room was empty except for a bucket in the corner that was clearly Fisher's idea of a toilet, and a few rusty old nails sticking out of the wall. She walked over to them. Maybe if she twisted her body just right and stood on tiptoes, she'd be able to use one of them to saw through her restraints.

She tried several times but couldn't get the angle right. On the last attempt, she slipped, and a nail tore into her flesh.

She cried out as a stabbing pain shot through her hand. Warm blood trickled onto the concrete floor. She considered the merits of dying from tetanus instead of thirst and decided both were heinous. She was about to give her escape attempt another try when the trap door rattled and creaked as it was opened.

An aluminium ladder appeared. Fisher climbed down, and Jayne considered trying a Krav Maga kick to his solar plexus, but with her hands tied behind her back, her balance would be off.

No, she needed to be smarter than that and think her way through rather than react in a rash manner.

"Awake at last, Jayne."

"What did you give me?"

Fisher shrugged. He placed a bottle of water and a sandwich on the floor. "Thought you might be hungry."

A surge of hope raced through her. If he'd brought her food and water, he might take her restraints off. "I am," she said, deciding to try a different tack. "That's very kind of you. Can you free my hands so that I can eat?"

Fisher barked out a single laugh. "Now, I know I'm not as smart as you, Miss Super-Lawyer, but I'm not completely stupid."

"Then how do you expect me to manage?"

"You'll figure it out." He began to leave, but then his eyes zoomed in on the blood spots on the floor. He grabbed her arm and turned her around. She winced as he poked at the tear in her flesh. He walked over to the nails and pulled them out one-by-one, slipping them into his pocket. He wagged his finger in front of her face. "Very sloppy of me."

Fisher began to climb up the ladder, and when he was about halfway, he glanced over his shoulder, a cruel tilt to his lips. "I'd love to stay and chat, but I'm afraid your boyfriend is expecting my call."

Jayne's heart jolted as he disappeared through the hole. The lock mechanism ground back into place.

She slumped to the floor, legs splayed out in front of her, which at least didn't cause too much pain to her shoulders. No more than a few minutes passed before Fisher returned. Jayne scrambled to her feet as he jumped off the last couple of rungs and came towards her, holding a mobile phone.

"Want to say hello to your boyfriend?" he said, waving the phone in the air, his tone taunting and arrogant.

Jayne lunged, but Fisher stepped away, and she stumbled and fell, scraping the skin off her knees on the concrete floor.

"Take it easy. You have to promise to be good first. Can you be good, Jayne?"

She glanced up at him and nodded, swearing that the first chance she got, she was going to nail this fucker in the balls.

"Good girl. Now stand over here by me. Otherwise, we won't get a signal."

She did as he asked. He wrapped his arm tightly around her waist, his fingers pinching her hip, and she did her utmost not to cower away from him. He smelt of stale sweat and cigarettes, and as the stench permeated her nostrils, she wanted to heave.

Her heart leapt when she heard Rupe's muffled voice.

"Rupe," she yelled, but was cut off when Fisher wrapped an arm around her throat and pressed hard. She began to gag.

"In a minute," Fisher said to her. "So, Whittingham, have you got my money and transport sorted?"

Jayne strained to hear what Rupe was saying, but Fisher had the phone too close to his ear.

"Good," Fisher spoke into the phone. "Right, I'm going to let you go, Jayne, but be warned: make a stupid move, and you'll regret it."

He dropped his arm from around her neck and moved it to her chest, holding her tightly against him. Revulsion rolled through her as Fisher held the phone up to her ear.

"Rupe," she managed to choke out.

"I'm here, babe," he said, his wonderful voice so soft and gentle. She bit back the tears that threatened to fall, knowing that if he heard how frightened she was, it would make things worse for him.

"Are you okay?" he said.

"Yes."

"We're going to find you. Trust me."

"I do." She bit her lip, as hot tears seared her eyes. "Rupe?"

"Yeah, babe. I'm still here."

Jayne took a deep breath and snapped her head backward,

cracking Fisher hard in the face. He grunted, fell to his knees, and dropped the phone. It skidded across the room. Jayne threw herself after it, crashing painfully to the ground.

"I'm underground," she shouted into the handset, the words tumbling from her lips. "It's got a tiny window, but I can't climb through. It's cold. There's a trap door, and he drops a ladder—"

Fisher hauled her to her feet and smashed his fist into her face. She screamed and crumpled to the floor as pain exploded in her head. She vaguely heard Rupe calling her name, but she couldn't force out any words in response. Her vision flickered, and she tasted the metallic tang of blood in her mouth. The room started spinning. She was going to pass out.

"That was very stupid," Fisher hissed. He kicked her hard in the abdomen, and she curled into a ball as blackness consumed her.

∽

Rupe almost slammed his phone into the wall but stopped himself just in time and punched it instead. The skin across his knuckles burst open, and blood seeped between his fingers.

"Open the app," Mike urged. "We've got him."

Rupe shook his head. "He was using a different phone. He's not as dumb as we first thought."

"So what does that mean?" Mike said in an irritated tone.

Rupe sank into a chair and covered his face with his hands. Jayne had been so brave, but her information was virtually useless without a trace. Oh God, what was Fisher doing to her right at that moment?

He stared at the floor. "We have to start over, trace the number, and hope the phone is switched on, but for all we know, he'll rotate through every phone call. It's like trying to hit a moving target."

Mike expelled a curt breath. "So you're giving up?"

Rupe's head snapped up, and he glared at Mike. "No, I'm fucking not. Just give me a goddamn minute to get myself together and plan the next move. Do you have any idea how hard that was for me to hear her voice, to sense her fear, and not be able to do a fucking thing to help her?"

Mike's face softened, and he rested a hand on Rupe's shoulder. "I'm sorry."

Silence stretched across the room before Rupe let out a low sigh. He rose from the chair he'd collapsed into and headed for the door.

"Where are you going?" Mike asked.

"To find Jayne," Rupe replied.

34

When Jayne regained consciousness, she was lying on her side, her knees curled up to her chest. She groaned and struggled to sit up. The burning sensation in her face was agonizing, and given the pain in her side from where Fisher had kicked her, she probably had some bruised or cracked ribs. But it had been worth it because she'd taken *control*. Yeah, she'd paid for it, but that didn't matter. She'd been able to tell Rupe something, and that had to be better than nothing. She prayed the information had been useful. As long as she was still alive, she had a chance of being saved. Or saving herself.

She staggered to her feet, her whole body aching from the chilly basement, the hard floor, and the beating Fisher had given her. God, these cable ties were excruciating. Her hands felt about twice their normal size, and she worried that she could lose them if her circulation got much worse. She had to find a way to get them off her. Maybe then, she'd be able to take Fisher by surprise and have a chance of escape. She searched her mind for any small piece of information that would help, but she came up empty.

Then, out of nowhere, she remembered a military documentary she'd watched with Kyle years before. She'd been bored senseless, although he'd been transfixed. Part of the documentary included a piece on escaping capture if you were taken as a prisoner of war and, specifically, how to break out of cable ties. Her body started to jangle with excitement. Yes, she remembered now. She just hoped she had enough strength left in her arms to do it.

Standing in the centre of the room, Jayne bent her body at a ninety-degree angle. She lifted her hands as high as she could behind her back—silently thanking all those hours spent doing yoga—and slammed them into her backside, hard. Nothing happened except an agonizing pain in her wrists so intense that tears sprang from her eyes. She bit her lip to stop herself crying out, in case Fisher was anywhere close by and heard her.

She had to try again. Steeling herself against the pain she knew was coming, she lifted her arms again. Slam! Nothing. A squeal of pain escaped her lips, and she hesitated, her ears straining for any sign of Fisher. When there was none, she raised her arms for the third time. They smashed into her bottom, and her hands sprang apart. The zip tie skipped across the concrete floor and came to rest by the pee bucket.

She clamped a hand over her mouth to stop herself yelling with joy. She'd done it! As the blood began to flow unrestricted, an agonizing feeling shot through her hands. She whimpered then clenched her jaw tightly. It had been worth it. Her hands were free, and now she had a chance of taking Fisher by surprise. But there was nothing in the cellar that she could use as a weapon, not since he'd removed the nails. She stared over to where the zip tie lay as an idea took hold.

If it worked, she had a chance of getting out of there.

If it didn't, she feared what Fisher would do.

As full feeling returned to her hands, the pain receded a little. Her fingers were badly swollen and a pretty nasty shade of purple, and she had deep imprints in her wrists where the cable ties had embedded themselves in her flesh. But her plan was in place. All she now needed was to wait for the opportunity to arise, and when it did, she'd be ready.

Now that she had a strategy to escape, Jayne was impatient to implement it. But as time passed with no sign of Fisher, her frustration escalated.

"Hey," she screamed, after hours had passed with no sign of him. "Hey, I need help here."

She paused, her ear tilted upwards for any sign that Fisher was coming. Or any sound at all. Nothing. She rubbed her painful wrists and paced the floor, partly to alleviate her angst and partly to help with her aching back. She drank the water and ate the sandwich Fisher had brought her before she'd spoken to Rupe. More hours passed. Tired, scared, and agitated, she slumped against the wall and dropped to the floor. Hugging her knees into her chest, she comforted herself by humming one of her favourite songs. Her eyelids drooped, and despite the ever-present fear, she drifted into a restless sleep.

She was awoken some time later by a faint scratching noise. Craning her neck, she listened carefully. Yes, there it was again. It sounded like someone shuffling. Stiff and sore, she clambered to her feet and shook out her arms and legs. The shuffling changed into the grinding sound of the trap-door bolt being opened. Springing into action, Jayne grabbed the bucket. Her eyes watered from the strong smell emanating from the plastic container. This was going to work. It had to.

She stood behind where he'd drop the ladder and waited. As the bottom rung hit the floor, Fisher began to climb down. When he was about halfway, he glanced over his shoulder. Taking her opportunity, Jayne hurled the contents of the bucket right into his face. Her shot was spot on. Fisher howled and pressed the heels of his hands to his eyes. Jayne grabbed the belt loop on his jeans and yanked hard. He lost his balance and fell off the ladder. As he crashed to the ground, Jayne lifted her leg and slammed her foot hard into his crotch. His piercing shriek was high enough to shatter glass, and he curled into a tight ball.

She threw herself up the ladder. She was almost at the top when she felt Fisher catch hold of her ankle. Jayne shook her leg hard and managed to free herself. She clawed at the earth, hauling herself up. As she turned around, Fisher was right behind her.

"No!" she yelled. She kicked out, catching him squarely in the chest. He plummeted back down with a howl. Jayne's heart crashed against her ribcage, and with trembling hands, she hoisted the ladder out of the hole.

"Oh, God, help me." She heaved the trap door over. It slammed shut. Jayne slid the lock into place before stumbling out into the night.

35

Jayne sprinted through the trees, the bark and broken twigs beneath her feet cutting painfully through her tender flesh. Her lungs screamed for a break, but her brain demanded that she keep on going. For all she knew, Fisher could be chasing her, and if he caught up with her, he'd kill her.

The woods were dense, the light from the full moon barely breaking through the foliage, and very quickly, Jayne became disorientated. She skidded to a halt, her ears straining for sounds of being followed. In the distance, an owl hooted. Jayne jumped, and she broke out in goose bumps. She rubbed her hands up and down her arms, even though it wasn't cold above ground. The summer night cast a mild breeze over her bare skin.

When she was fairly sure she was still alone, she began scanning the area for signs of a pathway. Paths led to roads—and roads led to help.

She lost track of time. As her body tired, she began to lose hope of finding her way out of the woods. If she weren't so scared, she'd wait for first light. At this time of the year, dawn couldn't be very far away. But no, she had to keep moving. If Fisher did manage to escape, the more she moved around, the less likely it was that he'd be able to find her.

And then another thought occurred to her: what else could be lurking in these woods? England might not rival Australia when it came to nasty critters, but she vaguely remembered a story about the growing number of what the press called "false widow spiders," which didn't sound like something she wanted to come into contact with, especially with no shoes on. And what about snakes?

With a renewed sense of urgency, she pressed on, but when a sharp pain shot through the sole of her foot, she cried out. Spotting a fallen log, she limped over and examined the damage as well as she could in the dim light. Blood coated her fingers, and her foot throbbed in agony. She wouldn't be able to tell how bad the injury was until the sun came up, but one thing she did know —she couldn't put any weight on it.

Her running curtailed, she limped through the trees, hot tears pricking her eyes. She would not cry. Tears would solve absolutely nothing, apart from diminishing what little she could see.

The burning sensation in her throat grew the more she moved, and her lips were dry and cracked. She tortured herself with images of cool streams and ice-cold drinks straight from the fridge.

Her thoughts turned to Rupe. She couldn't begin to imagine the torment he was going through. Not knowing where she was had to be driving him into a madness of sorts, and she knew— she just knew—that he'd be thinking the worst.

Jayne glanced upwards, and her heart leapt with hope. A faint glow was spreading across the sky. Dawn was breaking, and that meant she'd have a much better chance of finding her way out.

She spotted the trunk of a tree that had been felled, leaving behind a low stump. She realised she was wasting her time and what little energy she had left, and she decided to rest. Her eyes darted around, on the lookout for any signs that Fisher had miraculously managed to free himself. The common-sense side of her brain told her that he had no chance unless he'd built a secret door to the underground basement, which seemed beyond the realm of possibility. Those walls had been solid. She should know. She'd examined every inch.

Before the sun had peeked over the horizon, Jayne decided that she had enough light to start moving again. A quick glance at her foot revealed a two-inch gash in her heel. Blood had coagulated, but from what she could make out, it would definitely need stitches and a healthy dose of antibiotics.

Using only the ball of her left foot, she hobbled through the trees, and in the growing light, it didn't take her long to find a path. The weight of terror lifted from her shoulders, replaced by hope. Dragging her left foot behind her, ignoring the throbbing pain, she scampered as quickly as she could down the path.

A distant sound of an engine made her halt, her ears straining to figure out which direction it was coming from, but with the sound bouncing off the trees all around her, it was impossible to determine.

She cursed and set off once more. The farther she went, the louder the noise grew from what had to be a nearby road. With a silent whoop of excitement, she upped her pace, and after what seemed like an age, she saw a car speed past.

"Oh, please, please," she muttered as she spilled onto the road. She waved her arms about, but the car didn't stop, and eventually, it disappeared from sight. The road was little more than a small country lane, but surely, more cars would come. As that thought crossed her mind, she heard another car.

Taking a huge risk, Jayne stood in the middle of the road. She was conscious that she had to look a terrible sight, but if she gave this driver an opportunity to pass, they might take it.

As the car came into view, she began waving her arms again, and when it slowed and eventually stopped in front of her, she began to cry.

"Please," she said, scampering around to the driver's window to be met by the surprised and concerned gaze of a man in his early thirties. "Please help me."

"What's happened, love?" he said, climbing out of the car. When Jayne tried to speak, but found she couldn't, he gently put his arm around her and placed her in the passenger seat.

"Let's get you to hospital, okay?" He started the car and set off.

"Do you have a phone?" she managed to croak. "I need to call my boyfriend."

"Of course, love. It's in my briefcase." He pointed into the back seat. "Stops the temptation to answer it when I'm driving," he said with a grin.

Jayne unhooked her seatbelt and scrabbled around the back seat, eventually locating his phone.

"Where are we?" she asked.

"Not far from Challock." When she frowned, he added, "Kent Downs."

"Do you have any water?"

He gave her a pained look. "I'm sorry, love, I don't. We'll be at hospital soon though." Then, almost as an afterthought, he said, "I'd better call my boss."

With a shaking hand, Jayne dialled Rupe's number. He answered on the first ring.

"Fisher," he snapped.

"Rupe, it's me," she cried. "I'm okay. I'm okay."

"Jayne!" His tone swam with relief. "Where are you? Oh God, where are you, babe?"

"I managed to get out. I'm in a car." She began to sob. "Someone stopped for me."

Her saviour gave her an embarrassed grin.

"Tell me where you are, Jayne. I'm coming to get you."

"I'm..." She turned to the man. "Which hospital are you taking me to?"

"William Harvey is probably the closest."

"I got that. I'll be there." Rupe hesitated. "Are you badly hurt?"

"I'm okay. Honestly. Just be there, please."

"I'm setting off right now."

Jayne began to cry softly as she hung up. She was safe. And despite the pain, the suffering, the fact that her foot was most likely infected and her ribs severely bruised—if not cracked—a possible broken cheekbone, and her desperation for a drink, a small smile stole over her face.

She had that fucker locked in his own tomb.

36

Rupe launched himself through the automatic doors of the emergency department with Mike at his shoulder. At the reception desk, a couple of young mothers with distraught kids perched on their hips were trying to explain to the overworked receptionists why their offspring were in the process of deafening the whole waiting area.

"I'm looking for Jayne Seymour," he said, ignoring the glares from the two mothers.

"If you'll just wait a moment, sir," the receptionist said. "I'm dealing with these ladies at the moment."

Mike stepped forward and flashed his badge at the mothers. "Sorry to interrupt, ladies," he said, giving them a warm, friendly smile. "Police business." His gaze turned to the receptionist. "Jayne Seymour?" he asked with a raised eyebrow.

The receptionist clicked her mouse several times. "Cubicle four."

Rupe took off. He drew back the curtain of the cubicle and inhaled sharply when he saw what that bastard had done to his girl.

"From the look on your face, I take it I'm out of this year's

Miss World competition." Despite the attempt at humour, her bottom lip wobbled.

As gently as he could, he drew her into his arms. "I'm here," he said, stroking her hair. "You're safe."

Jayne began to cry then. His tough-as-they-come, sharp-witted, and even sharper-tongued girl broke down in his arms and sobbed. Rupe met Mike's gaze and cocked his head. Mike nodded and stepped outside, pulling the curtain across to give them some privacy.

When she'd stopped crying, Rupe drew back and gently brushed a stray hair from her face. "What has the doctor said?"

She sniffed and dragged the back of her hand over her nose. "I've only been triaged so far. I need stitches in my foot, and he thinks my ribs may be cracked or at least very bruised. Same with my cheekbone. He'll know more after the X-rays."

Anger surged through Rupe. He wasn't the kind of guy who experienced such extremes of emotion, but after what Jayne had been put through by that bastard, he'd see Fisher in hell. His emotions must have been playing out on his face because Jayne squeezed his arm.

"I'm going to be okay. That's all that matters."

Rupe shook his head. "No, it's not."

"Hey," she said with a shake of his arm. "Rein in the alpha, okay?"

Despite the fury making his insides churn uncomfortably, he grinned. "I'll do my best." He tilted his head to one side. "Feel up to telling me what happened?"

She nodded. "Can you get Mike? He'll need to hear this."

Rupe stuck his head through the curtain and beckoned Mike over. They both pulled up a seat at Jayne's bedside while she filled them in on the last two and a half days. When she reached the part where she escaped, intense pride surged through Rupe. He'd always known Jayne was tough—it was one of the things he found so very attractive about her. But the way she'd dealt with the horror of being kidnapped, beaten, and scared for her life humbled him.

"So he's still underground?" Mike said when Jayne finished.

She shrugged. "I presume so, unless he's managed to get out, although I don't see how that's possible."

"Do you think you'd be able to draw us a map?" Mike asked.

"I can do better than that," Jayne said. "I'll show you personally, although I did wander around a bit in the woods, so it might take me a while to find the right spot. It'd be good if you could get helicopter support."

Rupe stiffened his spine. "You're not going back there."

Jayne gave a small smile. "Rupert, you know I don't react well to being told what to do."

Mike chuckled and bumped Rupe's shoulder. "I wouldn't argue if I were you. Besides," he added, "she won't be alone."

Rupe almost growled. "You've got that right."

∽

As the helicopter circled overhead, Jayne, Rupe, and Mike, along with a half-dozen other officers, set off through the woods from where the stranger had picked up Jayne earlier that day. Apprehension rolled through her system, but she needed to do this. For her sanity, she needed to see Fisher being led away in handcuffs. Being told about it after the fact wouldn't be the same balm to her ravaged psyche.

Word came through that the helicopter had located a clearing about half a mile ahead. As the group reached the spot, Jayne gripped Rupe tightly.

"There it is," she whispered, pointing at some wooden slats in the ground that were partially covered by twigs and leaves, which must have been blown across by the keen breeze. Off to the side was the discarded aluminium ladder. She was astounded at the memory of how she'd managed to keep her cool and drag the ladder out of the hole with Fisher launching himself at her.

Mike held up his hand. "Okay everyone, spread out, and wait for my orders. We don't know what he'll do when we open the hatch."

One of the detectives bent down to open the trapdoor. The heavy bolt scraped in the lock, and Jayne held her breath. As the detective shone a torch into the darkness, Jayne pressed forwards.

"Morning, fucker." Mike dropped the ladder into the hole. He motioned to the detective. "Go get him."

Jayne could feel Rupe vibrating beside her as Fisher emerged from the hole in the ground. She wrapped her hand around his waist and squeezed. Rupe's answering response was to shield her as Fisher was handcuffed, read his rights, and led away, but not before Jayne managed to meet his gaze. As he crossed in front of her, she stuck up her middle finger and mouthed, "Fuck you."

37

Jayne pulled her scarf more tightly around her neck and tentatively stepped outside. Slush covered the roads, the pristine white snow from a couple of days ago turned into a brown, slippery mess from the continuous footfall and traffic.

An incoming text beeped. She dug her phone out of her handbag and looked at the message: *All set.*

A broad smile spread across her face. *Perfect.* Everything was coming together nicely. She typed out a quick reply as another text came through, this time from Mike. Jayne frowned. Today was Fisher's sentencing hearing. A week ago, he'd been found guilty of kidnapping with intent and several other charges. She'd been back and forth about whether to go to the hearing, but in the end, with the help of her counsellor, she'd decided not to. She already had her closure. Whatever happened, Fisher was looking at significant jail time. She didn't need to hear the actual words spoken by the judge.

She opened the text. *Twenty-two years,* Mike had written. He'd added a smiling emoji on the end.

Jayne briefly closed her eyes as tension drained from her.

Twenty-two days was a long time to spend in prison for an ex copper. Twenty-two years would be torturous.

She pushed thoughts of Fisher from her mind. He didn't deserve another second of her attention, particularly today. She'd planned everything down to the last detail, and she wouldn't allow anything to spoil it.

She managed to flag down a taxi. As she closed the door on the bitterly cold February wind, a thrill ran through her, even if it was tinged with fear. She hoped to God she hadn't misread the situation. Well, there was only one way to find out.

Thirty minutes later, the cab pulled up outside Rupe's house. She paid the driver and jumped out.

Abi opened the front door, a wide grin on her face. She gave Jayne a hug. "Everything's here."

"Except Rupe, I hope," Jayne said.

"Oh, yes. Cash is delaying him until he gets your text."

"Great."

Jayne wandered to the back of the house and opened the door at the far end of the hallway. The smell of roses—white and pink—enveloped her, and she smiled. She stepped farther into the room. On a table in the centre, a bottle of champagne was chilling in a silver ice bucket, two crystal glasses placed on either side.

With a final check that everything was in place, she sent Cash a text: *Ready.*

She received one back almost immediately: *Five minutes.*

Her skin tingled as excitement surged through her. She began to pace as she watched the second hand tick on her watch. The slam of the front door echoing down the corridor made her pulse jump. *Okay, this is it, Jayne.*

"Will you stop shoving me and tell me what the fuck is going on?" she heard Rupe say.

"Just get in there, Witters," Cash replied, making Jayne chuckle under her breath.

The door opened, and Cash pushed Rupe inside. He gave Jayne a wink before closing the door behind him.

Rupe's mouth fell open the minute he'd stepped into the drawing room, and his expression remained stunned as Jayne walked across to him.

"Sorry for the cloak-and-dagger." She curved her hands around his face and kissed him. Rupe leaned into her kiss before pulling away.

"Well, this is a nice surprise," he said with a grin. "Although you pinched the flowers idea from me."

Jayne laughed. "I've never been very original."

Rupe tilted his head to the side. "Want to tell me what's going on?"

"Fisher got twenty-two years."

Rupe sucked in a breath. "You went?"

Jayne shook her head. "Mike texted me."

"And how do you feel?"

She shrugged. "I'm not sure I feel anything. I'm just glad he's no longer a part of our lives."

"So that's what the flowers and champagne are for? A way of putting the past behind us and looking to the future?"

"Got it in one," Jayne said with a smirk. "Well, that, and this..." She dropped down on one knee and held out a small velvet box. Inside nestled a gold signet ring she'd had engraved with their initials.

As surprise flitted across his face, she grinned. "Now, I know this isn't the done thing, especially for an old cad like yourself, born fifty years too late, but I also know that with everything that's happened to me over the last few months, you wouldn't want to push. So I'm asking you instead. Will you marry me?"

Rupe sank down onto his haunches until he was at eye level with her. He gripped her by the shoulders and eased her to her feet. A jolt of panic shot through her. A grave expression crossed his face, one usually reserved for when things were really dire.

"I mean you don't have to, and I totally understand if—"

Rupe placed a single finger over her lips. "Shush. Wait here."

He disappeared into the hallway, and Jayne sank into the nearest chair before her legs gave out. She'd made a horrid mistake. Rupe *was* old-fashioned, in so many ways, and given his less-than-enthusiastic response to her proposal, she clearly should have waited for him to ask first.

Rupe returned a few minutes later, one hand stuffed into the front pocket of his jeans. Then he held out his other hand and helped her to her feet. He flicked a lock of hair over her shoulder and then caressed her cheek.

"You're right. I am old-fashioned, *especially* when it comes to asking the woman I love to marry me." He held his palm towards her. On top was a black velvet box, almost identical to the one she'd presented to him. "I bought this months ago. I wanted to be prepared for when you were ready. I guess that time is now."

His eyes were full of tenderness as he opened the box. Inside was an oval-shaped diamond surrounded with tiny sapphires. Tears welled up behind Jayne's eyes as Rupe slipped it onto her finger. He held out his hand for her to do the same to him. He touched his palm to her cheek. "I know what a tough few months it's been. I know you like people to believe that time didn't fuck you up, but I also know you, Janey. That's why I waited." He leaned down and brushed his lips against hers. "That's a yes, in case you're wondering."

Jayne laughed. "You had me worried for a moment."

He pulled her into his arms and rested his forehead against hers. "I never thought I'd feel grateful for being charged with murder, but if I hadn't been, then I wouldn't have found you."

Jayne wrapped her arms around his neck. "I'm not an easy person to live with. I'm a workaholic, I constantly bring my cases home with me, and I get far too embroiled in the lives of my clients."

Rupe grinned. "I don't mind competing for your time and

affection." He ran the tip of his nose down hers. "But you should know that I will play dirty to make sure I win."

Jayne pulled him down for a kiss. "I was rather hoping you'd say that."

THE END

CASH
A WINNING ACE SHORT STORY

GRAB YOUR COPY FREE WITH SIGN UP TO MY READER GROUP

Don't let appearances fool you...

Tennis ace Cash Gallagher has it all—money, fame, adoration

Women want him.

Men want to be him.

But for Cash, it's not enough.

Something is missing.

And if he doesn't figure out what, he may lose his mind.

Read the short story prequel to Winning Ace, and get a sneak-peak into Cash's life before Tally

WINNING ACE
(THE WINNING ACE SERIES BOOK 1)

Does Tally McKenzie want the man?
Or the story?

She can't have both.

Tally's driven. She loves being a reporter. All she needs is a big break. When it comes, she won't miss it.

Cash dominates centre court. Outside tennis, he keeps everyone at arms length, especially the press. What if they discover his secret?

Tally, though, gets through, and there's a spark... a hot, burning spark.

He trusts her. Was it a mistake?

Will she betray him?

Her heart wants love—and the promotion.

Which will she choose?

To find out, grab your copy of Winning Ace, the first book in the Winning Ace series at Amazon today.

LOSING GAME
(THE WINNING ACE SERIES BOOK 2)

Cash and Tally return in the sizzling sequel to Winning Ace

Are some relationships broken beyond repair?

Hurt at her lover's betrayal, Tally flees to Brighton and tries to pick up the pieces of her shattered life.

Stubborn to the last, Cash tracks her down and confesses his darkest secret.

His honesty wins her back—but will it cost him his career?

Can their deepening relationship survive all the challenges?

Or is the hot tennis ace about to discover his dark past is the least of his woes?

**Buy your copy of Losing Game at Amazon now!
and find out if love conquers all.**

GRAND SLAM
(THE WINNING ACE SERIES BOOK 3)

The captivating finale to the Winning Ace series

A destroyed career.
A bitter break-up.

After Tally's perfect life implodes, she moves to Greece. There she finds a country overcome with refugees fleeing the crisis in the Middle East.

She vows to help and, in the process, begins to heal herself.

Shattered by his loss, Cash commits to months of therapy, determined to win back the love of his life. His struggles, though, are far from over.

When a shocking turn of events thrusts Tally back into Cash's life a moment of joy brings a stranger into their lives.

Who is she? What does she want?

And will her arrival signal the end of Tally and Cash's hard-fought happiness?

Grand Slam has the answers readers have been waiting for. Grab your copy at Amazon today.

FROM MY HEART

Thank you so much for reading Mismatch. That you've given your precious time to read my novel means more to me than I'll ever be able to express.

Mismatch was borne from various readers begging to hear more about Rupe Fox-Whittingham after reading books one to three of the series, and so I could hardly refuse their requests! Besides, Rupe really deserved his own story, as well as a happily ever after of his own. This novel was such fun to write. Rupe is a fantastic character to spend time with. I had a real blast!

I'd love to hear what you thought of Mismatch. Please feel free to get in touch via email, Facebook, Twitter or by signing up to my reader group

Would you consider helping other readers decide if this is the right book for them by leaving a short rating on Amazon? They really help readers discover new books.

Next from me is a standalone novel called My Gift To You, which is due for release in March 2018. I hope you love it as much as I do.

ACKNOWLEDGMENTS

My thanks to my writing mentor, Beth Hill, a wonderful lady without whom, I wouldn't be where I am today.

To Incy—thank you, thank you, thank you. Your generosity never fails to amaze me. I don't know what I'd do without you.

To Louise. My Rock. You're so very special to me. Thank you for everything you do. I don't have the words to express my gratitude.

To my ARC readers. You guys are amazing! You're my final eyes and ears before my baby is released into the world and I appreciate each and every one of you for giving up your time to read—and point out the odd errors that slip through the net!

To my fabulous street team whose efforts do not go unnoticed. In no particular order - Loulou, Jules, Niamh, Lindsey, Del, Michelle, Kay, Dawn, Linda, Demei and Ana Irenea. We may be small, ladies, but we're fierce! Hugs and kisses to each and every one of you

And last but not least, to you, the readers. Thank you for being on this journey with me.

If you have a couple of minutes, would you consider leaving a short review on Amazon? Reviews really help readers discover new books, and they're particularly important for up and coming authors. You'd be helping more than you know

ABOUT THE AUTHOR

Tracie Delaney writes contemporary romance novels that centre around strong characters and real life problem with, of course, a perfect Happy Ever After ending (even if she does sometimes make her characters wait a little while!)

When she isn't writing or sitting around with her head stuck in a book, she can often be found watching The Walking Dead, Game of Thrones or any tennis match involving Roger Federer. Her greatest fear is running out of coffee.

You can chat with Tracie on Facebook (www.facebook.com/traciedelaneyauthor) or Twitter (twitter.com/tracie_delaney), or, for the latest news, exclusive excerpts and competitions, why not join her reader group (smarturl.it/lvtnjm) and those things will be automatically delivered right to your inbox, along with a special gift just for signing up.

Tracie lives in the North West of England with her amazingly supportive husband and her two crazy Westie puppies, Cooper and Murphy. Any tips on stopping them chewing the furniture would be gratefully received.

Tracie loves to hear from readers. She can be contacted through her website at
www.traciedelaneyauthor.com

Printed in Great Britain
by Amazon